John Esten Cooke

Out of the Foam

A Novel

John Esten Cooke

Out of the Foam
A Novel

ISBN/EAN: 9783337001803

Printed in Europe, USA, Canada, Australia, Japan

Cover: Foto ©Andreas Hilbeck / pixelio.de

More available books at **www.hansebooks.com**

OUT OF THE FOAM.

A Novel.

BY

JOHN ESTEN COOKE,

AUTHOR OF

"HILT TO HILT," "HAMMER AND RAPIER," "FAIRFAX," "SURRY OF
EAGLE'S NEST," ETC., ETC.

NEW YORK:

Carleton, Publisher, Madison Square

LONDON: S. LOW, SON & CO.

MDCCCLXXI.

Stereotyped at the
WOMEN'S PRINTING HOUSE,
Corner Avenue A and Eighth Street
New York.

CONTENTS.

PART I.

THE ATTACK ON WESTBROOKE HALL.

PART II.

THE BLOOD-HOUND.

OUT OF THE FOAM.

PART I.

THE ATTACK ON WESTBROOKE HALL.

CHAPTER I.

THE BEACON.

ON a stormy night of autumn, a boat, approaching from the open sea, drew rapidly near the coast of Pembrokeshire, the most western of the shires of Wales.

The coast was wild, rock-bound, jutting out into gigantic headlands, and lashed by the restless surges of St. George's Channel, breaking with a hollow murmur on dangerous reefs. At the point which the boat approached, the loftiest of these headlands rose precipitously from the foam; at its foot grinned the jagged teeth of rocks which had wrecked many a vessel; and in the cavernous recesses the long bellow of the waves was mingled with the shrill scream of the sea-fowl.

The boat was rowed by four men, and in the stern stood a fifth personage wrapped in a cloak.

The stars, glittering from moment to moment, between the masses of black cloud, scarce revealed the dusky figures; but all at once there shot up from the headland, towering at a dizzy height above, a pillar of flame, which threw its crimson glare far out upon the waves of the channel.

Every instant the fiery streamer grew more brilliant. The wind began to blow big guns, and the gigantic torch flickered in the gusts. The boat flew on, — was steered through the threatening reefs by the man in the stern, — and finally shot straight toward the perpendicular precipice, where it seemed impossible to land.

The steersman, however, evidently knew the locality. All at once, there appeared a sort of indentation in the precipice, from which a winding pathway was seen to ascend the cliff. The boat touched land, or rather the rock; the man in the cloak leaped ashore, carrying under his arm a black leather valise; and the boat, without delay, returned toward the open channel.

As it moved away, the man in the cloak said, in the brief tone of command, —

" Remember my orders, men. Return to this spot every night, for ten nights, at this hour. The corvette will stand for the coast of Ireland, but regularly beat up again at nightfall. My business may be finished in two days; if not in ten, I will be dead."

And the speaker rapidly ascended the cliff by the rugged path, which, in twenty minutes, conducted him to the plateau on which streamed the beacon light.

It was a great bonfire in a fissure of rock, not far from a sort of hut leaning against a mass of granite. On a bench, in front of the hut, sat a woman of about fifty, clad in sad-colored garments, and looking out thoughtfully upon the channel. The face of this woman was pale and emaciated; her hair was sprinkled with gray; and from time to time she passed backward and forward through her fingers the beads of a Catholic devotee, attached to her girdle. Poor as her dress and surroundings were, there was something proud and imposing in her appearance. In the full glare of the beacon light every detail was plain.

The man drew near. At first the crackling

of the fire and the dense smoke made the woman unaware of his approach. All at once, however, he stood beside her, and exclaiming " Edmond ! " she rose to her feet.

" Mother ! " came in response, and a moment afterwards she was locked in the man's embrace.

As he extended his arms his cloak fell, and he was seen to be clad in the full uniform of a captain of the French navy.

This scene took place nearly a century ago, and England and France were then at war.

CHAPTER II.

THE SOLITARY WOMAN AND HER VISITOR.

THE young officer and the woman sat down side by side on the bench, in the full light of the beacon fire.

The light revealed his face and figure clearly. He was about twenty-five; of slight figure, but evidently active and powerful. The face was bronzed by sun and wind. In the black eyes, keen and piercing, could be read force of character, and a courage as cool as it was reckless.

They talked long and earnestly. The sailor seemed to be narrating his adventures.

" And now, mother," he at length said, "since I have finished with myself, let us come to yourself. You still keep up your beacon ?"

" Yes, yes, my son ! " was the reply, in French,

the language of their conversation. " Alas ! it is little to do in expiation of my sins."

" Your sins ? "

" My great sins. Do not bring them to my memory. That beacon, you know, warns vessels approaching the reefs. It has saved many lives."

" True, mother — mine among the rest. I dared not look for a pilot, and your beacon saved the corvette last year."

" A whole year since your last visit ! "

She gazed at him tenderly as she uttered these words.

" Could I help that, mother ? England and France are enemies now, and the coast is guarded. A frigate may blow my little corvette out of the water at any moment."

" But you come — "

" On secret service."

" Tell me of it."

He shook his head.

" That is impossible, mother."

" And yet I tell *you* all ! "

He looked at her with a smile, and then shrugged his shoulders.

" You tell me nothing. What is it you have ever told me ? Stay : what brought you hither, many years since, to this solitary spot? Why did you leave beautiful France for this rockbound shore? Why do you live the life of a recluse, going to the fishing village beneath only once in many months to buy scanty supplies, with the poor little gold I brought?"

Her head sank.

"True," she said, "I have preserved silence as to all this, but only because I was compelled to do so. Believe me, Edmond, I have good reasons for my silence."

"And I too, my mother, for mine, namely, my orders. So we will respect each other's secret. Instead of speaking, I wish you to speak. Is a certain Viscount Cecil in this neighborhood now?"

"I do not know, my son."

"A certain Sir Murdaugh Westbrooke?"

The woman turned her head suddenly.

"I believe so. But your business with *him*, my son?"

The sailor uttered a short laugh.

"Merely to have an interview with him, my mother."

The woman shuddered.

"What is the matter, mother?"

"Beware of this man, my son."

" Beware of Sir Murdaugh Westbrooke ? "

" He is a terrible person, they say ; bloody and cruel ; and strange stories are told of him."

" Ah ! what stories ? "

" Mysterious things are said to take place at Westbrooke Hall. People speak of singular noises heard there, — of groans ; of great hounds prowling around ready to tear down intruders. More still, — it is said that a singular odor fills the house."

" A singular odor ? "

" The smell of corpses."

And the woman crossed herself.

The young sailor repeated his short laugh.

" That is mysterious, and curious, and I will go and see for myself. Groans — hounds — noises — the smell of corpses ! That is queer, and excites curiosity. But we have conversed sufficiently of the excellent baronet. Besides, I am in haste, my mother — I must leave you. First, however, here is some gold."

And he drew a heavily filled bag from his valise, and placed it in the lap of the recluse.

" Do not refuse it," he added ; " it is honestly earned ; and money is a friend, mother — one of the best in the world, and we should not repulse friends. Now I must hurry. I have some distance to travel to-night, and must change my costume."

With these words the sailor raised the valise, and entered the door of the hut, leaving the solitary woman still seated on her bench, in the light of the beacon fire.

This light streamed through the small window, and revealed a rush-clad floor, one hard wooden chair, a low narrow bed, with a poor but neat covering, and several exquisite engravings of scenes in the lives of the saints.

In ten minutes the sailor reappeared. He was scarce recognizable. His uniform had been replaced by a handsome dark travelling suit of English fashion; in one hand he carried a small travelling satchel, and in the other what appeared to be a bundle of rods about three feet in length, wrapped in shining oil-cloth.

"You behold, my mother, the gentleman tourist, Mr. Delamere," he said, laughing. "Let it be pardoned the captain, Edmond Earle, sailor, if he adopts the name of Delamere — *de la mèr* — as that to which he is best entitled after his own."

"And you will leave me, my son, so soon after gladdening my poor old eyes with your coming?"

"I must, mother; but do not fear: I will soon return."

"But the danger."

"Danger! Well, we are old acquaintances, this same danger and myself. We have shaken hands often, and I am not afraid of him."

"If they discover you—"

"They will arrest and hang me as a spy? Yes: but they will not probably discover me. I speak English like a native; and before they hang me, the town yonder will be blown to atoms by my cannon."

The recluse clasped her hands.

"Oh, my son! do not go."

He laughed grimly.

"Be at rest, my mother: there is no danger; and you will not behold that fine spectacle from your headland,—the coast of this good Pembrokshire raked by the guns of my corvette. See! yonder is her light on the horizon. She is standing out to sea. You do not see it? I am a sailor, and see far. And now, farewell, my mother. I will revisit you to-morrow night, I think. Embrace me."

And embracing the woman, the sailor set out rapidly by a path which led down the mountain side toward the interior.

CHAPTER III.

THE GYPSY.

A MILE southward from the headland which we have described, lay the fishing village of Oldport, an assemblage of huts, many of them consisting of the overturned hulls of wrecked vessels, in which lurked rather than lived openly a wild and lawless class of men, half fishermen, half smugglers, popularly known throughout the region as "The Wolves."

In front of a building of somewhat greater pretensions hung a rude sign depicting a cat with a bell around her neck. This was the inn of the *Cat and Bell*, and on the day after the scenes just described, a rickety old road-wagon, answering in place of a stage-coach, deposited at the inn the disguised French officer who had entered the vehicle at a town some miles distant.

Announcing himself as Mr. Delamere, tourist and amateur trout-fisherman, he dined; stated that he expected to remain some days; and taking from the oil-cloth case a jointed fishing-rod, fitted it together, and strolled through the village.

From the huts of the "Wolves," curious and threatening eyes were bent upon him, shining under shaggy masses of hair. The wild animals seemed to scent a popinjay in the well-clad amateur of their own trade.

But Earle did not see the scornful glances, or hear the threatening murmurs. He proceeded toward a body of wood, from which rose in the distance a great mansion of dark-colored stone; gained the wood, through which a stream ran, and rapidly following a path, muttered, —

"This leads to Westbrooke Hall — which is my object, since the worthy Viscount Cecil is not in the vicinity. I must reconnoitre. This is the path, I think —"

Suddenly he stopped. He had come upon a group of gypsies; an old crone in a red cloak bending over a blaze, two roguish-looking girls, and a young man, black-eyed, black-haired, lithe of figure, reclining at the moment between the girls, and picking his white teeth with a straw. He was a handsome young vagabond, and his ragged clothes did not conceal a graceful and vigorous figure.

No sooner had Earle made his appearance, than one of the girls rose and hastened to him.

"Shall I tell your fortune, handsome stranger?" she said.

Earle looked intently at the girl, shook his head, and replied in a strange tongue which seemed to produce an electric effect on the group. The girls started, the old crone turned her head, and the young man, rising to his feet, exclaimed, —

"How! you speak the Rommanye Rye! You are a brother?"

Earle replied in the same language, and the young man looked at him with astonishment.

"You speak the pure unmixed Rommanye Rye! Where did you learn it, brother, and who are you?"

"I learned it in Portugal, brother," responded Earle, "and am one of the tribe by adoption. Who I am, beyond that, is not important."

The gypsy came up close to him.

"Yes, it is important," he whispered.

"Why?"

" Because, if you are really a brother of the Rommanye Rye, — and you needs must be, since you speak our tongue, — I have something on hand in which you can help me, and yourself too."

" What is it ? and how will it benefit me ? "

" There will be ten thousand guineas to divide."

Earle looked sidewise at his companion.

" A robbery ? " he said, coolly.

The gypsy looked much shocked.

" Nothing of the sort, brother : the affair is a strange one ; but no robbery."

Earle found his curiosity much excited by this preamble, and said, —

" Well, tell me about it. I may be able to assist you."

The gypsy looked toward his companions, and whispered,

" Not here or now."

" When and where, then ? "

" Do you see that spot yonder, where the road skirts the dark pool, under the big rock, covered with trailing vines, hanging down in the water ? "

" Yes."

" Meet me there at midnight to-night. I

swear, on the faith of the Rommanye Rye, that no harm shall come to you!"

Earle laughed.

"I am not afraid," he said, "and I know that oath is sacred. I only demur to the time and place. I am at Oldport, and that is miles distant. Midnight is the hour to sleep; why not earlier and in a less secluded spot?"

"Because what I tell you must be told to you alone; and that spot is the place to tell it."

"Why?"

"You will discover."

Earle looked keenly at his interlocutor. He was evidently in earnest.

"You want my help?" said Earle.

"I must have help. None of the brothers of the Rommanye Rye are at hand. You are a stranger, but a brother. I will trust you. What do you say?"

"I say I will be yonder, near the pool, at midnight," was the reply.

And they returned to the group who had been eyeing them with ill-dissembled curiosity.

"This is a brother," he said to the gypsy girls. "There is no mistake about it."

The black-eyed houries showed their appreciation of the visitor, thereupon, by coming up to him, locking their arms, browned by the sun, around his neck, and kissing him with ardor.

The sailor laughed, and did not decline the ruddy lips. He then made a confidential gesture to the young gypsy, declined the offered supper, and went on, intent, it seemed, on making the circuit of the Westbrooke Park, until he reached the gateway.

This he soon found, — a huge arch, with carved stone abutments, — and, dragging open the ponderous affair, he entered the grounds.

They had been splendid, but were now returning to wilerdness. Hares ran across the road in front of the pedestrian, a deer disappeared in a tangled thicket, and no human being was seen, to indicate that the spot was inhabited.

All at once, Earle came in sight of a great building of age-embrowned stone, apparently dug from the neighboring quarries, with lofty gables, ivy-covered, and long rows of windows, close-shut, and giving no indication that the house was occupied by the living, whatever antics the dead might cut up, at midnight, in its suites of deserted chambers. The great front door was as closely secured, and a huge knocker in bronze scowled fiercely through cobwebs. In the circle in front of the portico, whose tesselated floor was giving way, was a stone urn, slowly crumbling.

Westbrooke Hall was not a cheerful spectacle.

Earle was looking at it, leaning, as he did so, against a tree, when a rough voice near him said, in a threatening tone, —

"Well, what is your business here?"

CHAPTER IV.

THE ODOR OF DEATH.

EARLE turned quickly.

Standing near him was a man of low stature, but herculean limbs, with a shaggy beard, bloodshot eyes, over which the brows were bent in a dark scowl, and holding in his hand, finger on trigger, a heavy carbine.

Beside him stood two large wolf-hounds, ready to spring. The man with this ferocious body-guard seemed reluctant to await Earle's reply before firing upon him.

The sailor exhibited little surprise and no fear.

"My business here?" he said. "Who are you that ask that? The gamekeeper?"

"Yes—who are *you?* I am told that suspicious characters are prowling about. Your name and business here, or I carry you before Sir Murdaugh!"

Earle reflected for a moment, muttering, —

"That would not be so bad."

The gamekeeper cocked his gun, scowling ferociously.

"Do you intend to answer me?"

"No."

"Then come along before his honor. He will find out who is prowling around his house."

Earle coolly nodded, and walked with the man toward the mansion. Reaching the front door, his companion drew from his pocket a huge key, opened the ponderous door, which grated on its hinges, and ushered Earle into a funereal apartment, hung round with old portraits, after which he disappeared.

The furniture was ancient and mouldy; and to add to this depressing influence, Earle's attention was speedily attracted by a peculiarly acrid, offensive, and even sickening odor, which he could compare to nothing but that issuing from some vault or charnel-house.

In spite of his courage and buoyancy of temperament, he shuddered. This funereal mansion, full of shadows and mystery, affected unpleasantly even the rough sailor.. The dim eyes of the portraits followed him, the brows scowled, the terrible odor, which he perceived now, came to perfect the depressing and melancholy influence of the place.

"Really, I have blundered into a vault," he muttered. "Some corpse is going to glide in at that door there, and clutch me by the hair!"

Suddenly a harsh and metallic.voice, almost beside him said, —

"Your business here? How did you gain entrance?"

Earle turned and saw before him a strange figure. In the new-comer's appearance there was something at once grotesque and terrible. He was a man of about sixty; of great height: gaunt, bony, with glittering eyes, deeply sunken under heavy brows, and a nose resembling the beak of a hawk. From the corners of a large and sensual mouth, protruded two tusks, rather than teeth. The result of this, was a permanent and ghastly sneer, which put the finishing touch to a physiognomy which excited at once fear and disgust — the sentiment of the ridiculous and the terrible.

He was clad in an old faded dressing-gown, the sleeves of which were rolled up, and had evidently not expected a visitor.

"Your business here?" he repeated, in his cold, forbidding voice, the muddy gray eyes rolling in their cavernous sockets.

Earle gazed at him coolly, and replied, —

"Your gamekeeper conducted me hither. I say *your* gamekeeper, as I presume you are Sir Murdaugh Westbrooke."

"I am."

As he spoke, the shaggy-headed Hercules entered. His master turned to him with a scowl.

"I ordered no one to be admitted here without my knowledge — why have you disobeyed me?" he said.

"It was long ago — I was wrong Sir Murdaugh," stammered the man.

"In future obey me," grated the metallic voice; "who is this — gentleman?"

The word seemed forced reluctantly from him.

"I am a tourist," said Earle, "travelling on my own affairs. I came to look at Westbrooke Park, and have been gratified with a view, also, of the interior of your residence, sir, — in the character of a vagrant brought up before your honor."

And Earle looked around him coolly. A door led from the apartment toward the servants quarters'—through folding doors, leading to a second receiving room, a window was seen open in rear, and through this window, the foliage of the park.

"Good!" muttered the sailor; "that is all I wanted to know."

He rose and bowed.

"If I am not to be committed as a vagabond, I will now take my leave, sir," he said.

Sir Murdaugh Westbrooke, bowed stiffly.

"Before I take my departure, however, may I ask one question, sir?" said the sailor.

"Ask it."

"It may appear intrusive."

"Ask it!" grated the voice.

"Since you so politely permit me, I will venture to ask," said the sailor, coolly, "what the very peculiar odor I perceive here is due to, Sir Murdaugh."

The baronet drew back and seemed to freeze. Only his eyes burned in their bloodshot recesses.

"Your question is offensive!" he growled.

"Then it resembles the smell I perceive."

And Earl snuffed up the air with manifest disgust.

" I compliment you upon the power of your imagination ! " sneered the baronet.

" My nose is the organ affected, and I should say that you have a corpse for a visitor at present, sir," said Earle. " But I grow really intrusive now, and will take my leave. Good-evening. Thanks for the hospitalities of Westbrooke Hall. We shall probably meet again."

And he bowed and left the apartment. As he did so the baronet called, —

" Wilde ! "

The shaggy gamekeeper was at the door, and quickly made his appearance.

" Follow that man and find out where he goes, and who he is — I do not like him. There is something in his face and voice that warns me to beware of him. Who is he ? You do not know ? Why do you not know ? What do I employ you for ? Go, I say, and track him, and bring me word all about him ! "

The man, sullen but cowed, went out, and the baronet looked toward the door through which Earle had disappeared.

"If that man comes here again with his talk about odors and corpses," he muttered in his harsh voice, while the yellow tusks protruded threateningly, "I will make a corpse of *him!*"

CHAPTER V.

THE RENDEZVOUS.

IT was nearly midnight: the moon had risen about half an hour before, and its pallid light revealed every feature of the lonely and lugubrious locality fixed upon by the gypsy for his rendezvous with Earle.

. Nothing more gloomy and forbidding than the spot in question could be imagined.

The road, or rather bridle-path, indicated by the gypsy, ran along the steep banks of the stream we have spoken of, and near a dark and sullen-looking pool above which rose a huge rock, festooned with spectral-looking vines, and covered nearly with dense foliage. The stream, merrily brawling on elsewhere, here ˙dragged its black and sombre current slowly along, and deposited its froth and scum. Above the pool a dead bough, gnarled and abrupt, resembled the gaunt arm of some fiend stretched out — beneath, on the sullen water, the shadows assumed ghostly and threatening outlines.

It was a spot to commit a murder, not to hold a midnight interview in, save with the hand upon some weapon. The very hooting of a great-horned owl, buried in the leaves, sounded unearthly. The spot seemed given up to gloom and the recollection, by the very inanimate objects, of some terrible tragedy.

Precisely at midnight, a figure wrapped in a cloak approached the great gnarled tree near the rock hanging over the pool, and the moonlight clearly revealed the form of Earle.

"Well, I am here," he muttered; "where, I wonder, is my friend of the black eyes?"

"Here!" came from the shadow of the rock.

And the gypsy advanced into the moonlight.

Earle advanced in his turn. Under his cloak his hand grasped the hilt of his poniard.

They faced each other directly opposite the pool; and the dark eyes of the gypsy, full of wary cunning, were fixed upon the calm face of Earle.

"I see you are a brave man, brother," he said.

"How have I proved that?" said Earle.

"By coming here at an hour like this, alone."

"That is no proof of my courage. You are but one man — I am another."

The gypsy laughed.

"And a cool one. Others might have refused this meeting. This spot has a black reputation in the neighborhood."

"Why?"

"A man was tied to that tree, and lashed nearly to death."

"Indeed!"

"And six feet from it, another was murdered, and his body dragged to the pool yonder, where it was thrown in, with weights to hold it down."

"How do you know that?"

"I saw it."

"You saw the murder?"

The gypsy nodded.

"Why did you not denounce the murderer? But doubtless you did so."

The gypsy shook his head.

"I was too intelligent for that."

"Too intelligent?"

"Yes."

"Explain.'

The gypsy laughed again. It was a low, subtle sound, like the hiss of a serpent.

"Why should I have informed on the murderer?" he said. "No: I was too intelligent for that! A man is murdered; his body concealed in that black-looking pool; no one knows of the murder save the man or men who committed it, and a wandering vagabond of a gypsy who chanced to be in the copse yonder, and witnessed all,—and you ask now why the vagabond did not go to a magistrate and tell all; why he did not say, 'I saw another commit this murder.' No—I am acquainted with these good English justices of the peace. They demand a murderer where murder has been done—what more natural than the arrest of *the vagabond?*"

Earle nodded.

"You are right. And you held your tongue?"

"Yes."

"Knowing all?"

"Yes."

"Tell me what happened. There is nothing

like understanding all the particulars of a given event."

" The story is short. I will conceal nothing —for you are a brother of the Rommanye Rye, and the oath of the brotherhood seals the lips —·you know that."

" Yes."

" What happened was this: There was a man who had an enemy. That enemy met the man one day at this spot, seized him with the aid of a servant, bound him to that tree there, and lashed him as men lash a hound. I do not know why — enough that he lashed him till his flesh was bloody. Then the two went away and left him tied; when some passer-by found him he was nearly dead."

" That is a strange story," said Earle; "and this led to the murder?"

" Yes. The man who had been lashed got well, and waited. One day he was riding along this road just at dark with a mounted attendant. He met his enemy — the one who had treated him as I have described. I was yonder in that thicket, as I told you. The enemies met face to face, and he who had been lashed smiled sweetly, held out his hand, and said, 'I forgive you; my punishment was just.' At these words, the other held out his hand in turn. A minute afterwards he fell from his horse with a deep groan — the man whom he had lashed had stabbed him to the heart."

"Good!" said Earle; "there is a regular murder."

"Yes. The man did not die at once, so his enemy and the attendant dismounted and beat out his brains. They then fastened rocks, with their stirrup leathers, to the feet of the corpse, and dragged it to the pool yonder, where they threw it in, and it sunk to the bottom."

Earle listened with attention.

"And you saw all this?"

"Yes."

"And did not inform on the murderer?"

"No."

"Then the murder remained unsuspected?"

"On the contrary, it was discovered at once."

"How was that?— you interest me."

"The murdered man had been followed by a very fine blood-hound, a pet dog with him. When he was stabbed, the dog leaped at the throat of the murderer."

"Brave dog!— and they did not kill him too?"

" No : he escaped, and led the way afterwards to the spot where his master had been murdered. The marks of a struggle were found — the blood-stains on the grass over which the body had been dragged, and at last the body itself, in the pool where it had been sunk."

Earle reflected for some moments and then said, —

" That is a singular history you relate, brother, and yet your voice tells me that it is true. Now, what is your object ? To bring the murderer to justice ? "

The gypsy smiled.

"I should like to do so if I could, brother; but I cannot, being a vagabond; and then, I cannot afford it."

" Afford it ? "

" The secret is worth much money. Listen : I go — that is, you and I go — to the man who committed that murder and say, " Your life is in my hand; you killed a man ; pay me ten thousand guineas as the price of my secresy ? " That is plain, is it not ? "

Earle nodded coolly.

" Then we will divide the sum he pays us," said the gypsy.

"That would be liberal," returned Earle.

"You consent?"

"That depends. We have used no names; let us come to that. Who was the murdered man?"

"Giles Maverick, a prominent gentleman of Pembrokeshire."

"The murderer?"

"Sir Murdaugh Westbrooke."

CHAPTER VI.

E had scarcely uttered the words, when a low growl in the copse near them was suddenly heard; and an instant afterwards the gypsy sprung in the direction of the sound, which resembled the noise of rapidly retreating footsteps.

The gypsy followed with long leaps, like a wild-cat in pursuit of his prey; but in spite of all, the sounds became more and more indistinct, and suddenly ceased. The concealed personage had escaped.

Earle had remained motionless, leaning against the gnarled tree.

In ten minutes the gypsy returned to the spot, breathing heavily from his exertion.

" We have been tracked," he said, hastily.

Earle nodded.

" I thought so," he said.

" You thought so ? "

" Yes; that is to say, I feared as much."

" Why ? "

" I was at Westbrooke Hall late this evening, and had a conversation with Sir Murdaugh Westbrooke. As I went out, I heard him summon a confidential servant, or gamekeeper, whose name is Wilde. The man followed me, hung around the tavern at the village for an hour, disappeared, I thought; but now I find that he is a better hand at woodcraft than I am, a mere sailor. He has tracked me, and overheard all."

The gypsy knit his brow.

" You take it coolly, brother."

" There is no reason why I should take it otherwise."

" He will inform Sir Murdaugh."

" Of what ? "

" Of all he has heard."

" He has heard nothing."

" Nothing ! "

" We have been talking in the Rommanye Rye," said Earle.

The gypsy looked at him with admiration.

" That is true, brother," he said; " and you

have a long head on your shoulders. Now what is to be done?"

Earle reflected for an instant.

"The affair looks unpromising," he said; "but something may, perhaps, take place which will guide you in your business. The night is clear, we have some hours before us: why not pay a visit to the park of Westbrooke Hall, and try to discover, for one thing, whether I am mistaken in thinking that the man Wilde has tracked me? If I am right, he will return to make his report. Through a window chink we may overhear something; from a tree, which a good sailor like myself can easily climb, we may see something. Who knows? Let us try, at least."

And, followed by the gypsy, who evidently regarded him with admiration, Earle set out rapidly in the direction of Westbrooke Hall. In half an hour, they were near the boundaries of the park, which was encircled by a high wall.

As they drew nearer, they all at once discovered a light vehicle, to which a single horse was attached, standing in the shadow of the wall, at a point where the stones had partially fallen, and left a gap.

Through this gap two men were seen lifting

a third wrapped in a cloak, and apparently in the last stages of intoxication.

"Stand up, my hearty!" said one of the men, with a low laugh; "this way you have of going and getting yourself as drunk as a beast is not according to good morals, old fellow! There! use your legs and come on. Sir Murdaugh is waiting for you."

"Be quiet, and hush your gab, mate," said the other; "who knows who may be prowling about?"

"After midnight?"

"Yes. There are the gypsy people."

"Well, they *do* hate Sir Murdaugh."

"There, again. I have often warned you about calling names; stop it! Bear a hand there."

"You are right, mate. Come on, aged inebriate!"

And the two men half dragged, half carried the third along a path through the shrubbery, toward the hall.

Earle and the gypsy followed, walking noiselessly and keeping in the shadow.

As they approached the hall, a low growl from a kennel, where a hound seemed to be chained, greeted them, and a moment afterwards the door of the hall opened slightly, and revealed the figure of Sir Murdaugh Westbrooke, clad in his long dressing-gown, and holding a light in his hand.

Earle and the gypsy had reached the thicket near which the former had encountered the gamekeeper. In this they ensconsed themselves, and could see everything.

Sir Murdaugh shot a keen glance in the direction of the three figures.

"Make haste!" he said, impatiently.

"Come on, old gentleman!" muttered one of the men to the one between them.

The figure staggered, and would have fallen had not the two men held it up by main force. As it staggered, the hat fell off, the cloak dropped to the ground; and the light revealed all.

The figure was clad in a shroud, and the jaw had fallen.

It was a corpse.

CHAPTER VII.

EARLE laid his hand upon the arm of his companion. On the firm lips of the young sailor the moonlight revealed a sarcastic smile.

"Look!" he whispered; "there is the sort of goods in which our friend deals."

"Yes," said the gypsy, whose dark eyes were fixed upon the face of the corpse. "Is it another murder?"

"No."

"What?"

"I will tell you when there is less danger of being overheard."

In fact, the two men carrying the corpse had paused to listen. Something seemed to excite their suspicion.

"What is the matter?" came in low, harsh

tones from the lips of Sir Murdaugh West-brooke.

"I thought I heard a noise, sir," said one of the men.

"A noise?"

"In the thicket there." And releasing the arm of the corpse, the speaker took two steps toward the spot where Earle and the gypsy were concealed.

Earle laid his hand upon his poniard. The hand of the gypsy in like manner stole beneath his ragged jacket and grasped something—a knife, probably. There was no possibility of retreating. It was necessary, they felt, to await the attack and defend themselves.

But the danger quickly passed.

"Nonsense!" came in same low, harsh tones from the baronet; "all fancy! There is no one there. It is one in the morning. Bring in *that!*"

And with his long, lean finger he pointed to the corpse.

The man returned, muttering something, and again assisted his companion in dragging — for they rather dragged than carried — the body into the mansion. The lugubrious group with their funereal burden passed through the great doorway — it closed — save the glimmer through one of the windows, there was now no sign of life throughout the establishment.

"Well," said Earle, "we have stumbled upon something like an adventure. We did well in coming to visit the park. There is nothing like knowing the private affairs of a man you are to have dealings with!"

"Hist!" returned the gypsy suddenly. I heard a noise!"

"A noise? — Where?"

"In the wood yonder, behind the house."

Both listened. All at once footsteps became audible — the firm tread of a man, walking on the thick turf, which gave forth a muffled and dull response.

"He has arrived!" whispered Earle.

"Who?"

"The man who tracked me and overheard what was said yonder — Wilde?"

"He will discover us!"

"It is probable, as he has one of the hounds with him."

"Where is the dog?"

As he spoke, Wilde appeared in the moonlight, emerging from the shadow of the wood.

Beside him ran the great wolf-hound, nosing and uttering suppressed growls.

"What is the matter?" the man was heard to say in a low voice; "there is no one here, Wolf."

The dog continued his quest, uneasy, evidently, and more suspicious than his master.

"Come here," said Wilde; "you are losing your time. The first thing is to see Sir Murdaugh. Then we will come out and go the rounds, Wolf."

With these words he called the dog to him, and they disappeared behind the mansion.

"Now is the time to get off," whispered the gypsy.

"No: now is the time to discover more," returned Earle, coolly. "Go deeper into the thicket; no dog can find you there, if you lie down and keep quiet. I am going to the maintop to look out."

And with a short laugh, which revealed his white teeth, the young sailor emerged from covert, crossed the moonlit expanse in front of the house, and, climbing with the agility of a cat, an enormous oak whose foliage brushed the walls of the house, concealed himself among the leaves.

From the lofty perch which he had thus reached, and where he sustained himself by a firm grasp upon one of the lesser boughs, the young man could see into the establishment, one of whose window-shutters was open.

The apartment into which he looked was not that which had witnessed the interview between himself and Sir Murdaugh Westbrooke. It was a much smaller room on the left, plainly furnished. In the centre was a great arm-chair. Seated bolt upright in this chair, with grinning teeth, was the corpse.

Sir Murdaugh was standing erect, candle in hand. In his long dressing-gown, dark and draping his person from head to foot, he resembled a Roman augur, about to perform some mysterious rite. His face was pallid, and as he gazed at the body, the grin habitual with him distorted his features, revealing clearly the sharp tusks at the corners of his mouth. His sombre glance seemed to gloat on the lugubrious object. Earle shuddered almost. The effect produced by the expression of the pale face was that of the presence of one of the deadly cobras which the sailor had seen in the tropics — a mixture of fear and loathing.

The two men had retreated, hat in hand, to the door, and waited.

As Earle, from his hiding-place in the oak, took in the details of this singular tableau, the door opened and Wilde entered, followed by his wolf-hound.

CHAPTER VIII.

THE WOLF-HOUND.

THE baronet and the shaggy Hercules exchanged rapid glances.

Wilde made a slight movement of the head in the direction of the two men, and, as though comprehending at once the meaning of this sign, Sir Murdaugh Westbrooke pointed to the door, said something to the men, and they disappeared.

Wilde then rapidly approached his master. His face was dark and scowling. He spoke rapidly, with animated gestures, pointing, as he did so, in the direction of the pool near the boundary of the park.

As he spoke, Sir Murdaugh Westbrooke's face grew as black as night. His bushy brows were knit over his snake-like eyes, and he listened with unconcealed emotion.

The sailor, in his oak, uttered a low laugh.

"The worthy pair are discussing things," he said. "The man is telling his master of the mysterious interview between the mysterious stranger and the gypsy, at the pool. What will result? Let us look on, since it is impossible to listen."

The interview continued for about half an hour. Then the baronet was seen to point through the window toward the front of the house.

The sailor saw that gesture, and his marvellous acumen told him that Sir Murdaugh Westbrooke was informing Wilde of the supposed noise heard by the men when bringing in the dead body.

The Hercules turned quickly toward the door. As he did so, he made a sign to the wolf-hound, and the animal, as though understanding perfectly, disappeared at a bound.

A moment afterwards, Earle's attention was attracted by a low and continuous growling beneath the oak. He looked down and saw the dog coursing to and fro, and nosing the earth.

By a strange instinct, the wolf-hound paid no attention to the traces left by the men and their burden. Something seemed to draw him irresistibly toward the oak, in which Earle was concealed. Every circuit which he made brought him nearer; at last he reached the tree. His nose rested for a moment upon the trunk, and he snuffed at it in silence. Then his head rose, his dark eye glittered in the moonlight. He caught sight of Earle, half-lost in the foliage, and uttered a long, continuous, and furious bay.

As the deep and prolonged alarm issued from the hound's lips, Earle felt that he was lost. There was no possibility of remaining undiscovered: the hound had descried him; the hoarse bay could not be mistaken. It was the sound uttered by animals who have discovered their prey, and are furious to leap upon it, and tear it limb from limb. Earle felt that Wilde and the baronet would understand all in a moment, and throwing a rapid glance through the window, he saw that his fears were well founded

No sooner had the hoarse cry of the hound reached his ear, than the man Wilde started and turned toward the door.

Sir Murdaugh, who had gone toward the body, turned as quickly.

Wilde pointed in the direction of the sound, uttered some hasty words, and, drawing a hunting knife from his girdle, rushed from the room.

Earle saw that all was lost, unless he acted with decision. He did not hesitate. The inmates of Westbrooke Hall were persons, evidently, who did not fear bloodshed, and were apt to act without ceremony. Ilis life would in all probability pay the forfeit of his daring invasion of the precincts, and without a moment's hesitation Earle slid down the tree, passed from bough to bough, let his body fall from the lowest limb, and sprung upon the hound, who in turn darted at his enemy's throat.

Earle felt the hot breath of the animal on his face, and the sharp teeth touched his throat.

The struggle was desperate, but did not continue long. Before the teeth of the hound could close upon the throat of Earle, he drew his poniard, plunged it into the animal's body behind the shoulder, and hurling the dog from him, rushed into the thicket just as Wilde reached the spot, attracted by the last cry of the dying wolf-hound.

The Hercules uttered a growl so savage that it resembled that of a tiger. Drawing his knife, he hastened in the direction of a rustling which he heard in the thicket. Head down, like a mad bull, he burst through every obstacle, breathing heavily, uttering curses, his eyes glaring with rage.

But the noise receded — ceased. Coming to an open space, he saw through a vista two shadows clear the park wall and vanish.

Earle and the gypsy had effected their escape, and were lost in the great Westbrooke woods.

CHAPTER IX.

HOW EARLE STAGGERED AND FELL, UTTERING A CRY OF TRIUMPH.

A MORNING full of brilliant sunshine succeeded the night in which the events which we have just described took place.

It was one of those days of autumn which seem to make of the dull earth a fairy realm, all splendor, glory, and delight; when the forests blaze in orange, purple, crimson, and all colors of the rainbow; when the blue sky bears upon its bosom argosies of white-sailed clouds; and the sigh of the pines, the laughter of the breeze, the long and musical murmur of the waves, make up a symphony sweeter than ever Mozart, Verdi, or Rossini dreamed.

From the fishing village of Oldport, St. George's Channel was seen to roll its azure waves in the fresh breeze; and these blue billows as they reached the rocks in the small harbor, and at the foot of the gigantic headland, broke into snowy spray, which glittered in the sunshine.

Dotting the restless surface, covered with spangles, and growing more and more restless and brilliant as the breeze freshened, were a number of fishing-boats, with small triangular sails, which the wind filled, driving the barks rapidly before it.

As the morning drew on, the breeze freshened still more and more, and began to blow a gale; the fishing-boats were seen hastening landward; then as they approached they were tossed dangerously aloft; as they reached the shore, and were dragged up and rescued, the roughest water-dogs of the coast were evidently well pleased to be ashore, and not exposed in their small skiffs to the gathering tempest.

One sail-boat alone was visible now, beating up toward the headland.

This craft, even at a distance, was seen not to be a fishing-smack, but a pleasure-boat, gayly painted, and with ladies on board; for, as the boat veered and danced on the waves, her bright sides and the floating scarfs of women were plainly visible.

The wind grew stronger every moment, and in a group upon the strand, the rough " wolves," as the fishermen were called, watched the boat, which careened dangerously as it flew onward, making straight for shore.

" That much sail is enough to sink her," said a huge " wolf " in a ragged pea-jacket, and with hair growing down nearly to his eyes.

" The rudder is gone," said a calm voice behind the speaker.

The " wolf " turned round with a scowl. His eyes fell upon the neatly-dressed figure of Mr. Delamere, amateur fisherman.

" What are you a-saying there ?" he growled, contemptuously.

" I say," said Delamere, otherwise our friend the sailor, Earle, " that the rudder is gone, and the man in that boat is a sailor, who is steering her ashore with *his brains*, as he. has nothing else."

A low growl came from the " wolf."

" Look here, my hoppadandy," he said, turning to Earle and clenching his fist; " who are you that come here to larn old sailors their business ?"

He advanced threateningly upon the young man as he spoke. Earle did not move,

"Who are *you?*" shouted the "wolf," raising his arm to strike at him. "I'll smash your headpiece if—"

The sentence was not concluded.

Earle planted his left foot three feet in advance of him, followed rapidly with his right, and as the ball of the foot touched the earth his right fist darted out, backed by the whole weight of his body thrown with it, and struck the giant exactly where the low shag of hair terminated nearly between his eyes.

The "wolf" fell as though a battering-ram had struck him.

But, rising, stunned and dizzy, he rushed at his opponent.

In a minute he was down again. The rough crowd, whose sympathies had all been with their own representative, uttered a shout of admiration at the *amateur's* science. It was plain indeed that the slight stranger was a perfect master of the art of boxing, and his adversary, in spite of his size, was hesitating whether he should renew the attack or expend his remaining energies in violent curses, when a cry attracted the attention of every one—a cry so shrill and piteous that it thrilled through the roughest person present.

Earle glanced quickly in the direction of the cry, that is, toward the sea. That glance told him all. The sail-boat had run before the wind with the rapidity of a dry leaf borne onward by the breeze — had nearly reached the land; but at two hundred yards from shore had struck the reef, capsized, and a man and two women were seen clinging to the frail mast and the ropes, which rose and fell and beat upon the threatening surge.

The cry had issued from the women, and the crowd was instantly in commotion.

A boat was launched, and two of the "wolves" sprung into it. At fifty yards from the shore it capsized, and the men only reached land again by vigorous swimming.

A second attempt was made. In this case the boat swamped at twenty yards from shore.

A glance toward the overturned sail-boat showed that the strength of the young ladies — for such they were now seen to be — was rapidly deserting them. The waves beat them cruelly in the face, and tore at them. The wind roared at them, nearly wrenching the frail hands from the mast. The man, clinging to the gunwale, could afford them no assistance. In ten minutes, it was plain, they would desert their hold, and the surf would engulf them.

Suddenly, the crowd, who had been nearly paralyzed, was seen to divide.

In the open space, Earle was seen, without hat, coat, boots, waistcoat, or cravat, — a sailor in shirt and pantaloons, — with a hatchet in his belt and a rope the thickness of a man's finger tied around his waist.

" Stand back!" his clear voice rang out.

And throwing himself into the boiling mass, he struck out vigorously for the wrecked boat.

As he rose and fell like a cork upon the waves, the crowd shouted, following him with eyes of admiration. Every instant they expected to see him disappear, and held their breath as he sank in the hollows. As he rose again, swimming like a giant, the roar of voices sounded above the storm.

It is a splended spectacle to see man contending with the forces of nature. The sailor was defying the sea lashed to fury. The waves struck him with their huge hands, buffeting and howling at him — and he went on. The spray cut his face and filled his eyes, blinding him — and he went on. Hurled into the hollows of the billows, he rose like a leaf, cutting the foam. The crowd hurrahed, and held their breath, and ran into the sea, grasping the rope affixed to the sailor's waist.

Suddenly a shout, which seemed to drown the thunder of the wind, rose.

Earle had reached the boat and affixed the rope to a ring in the ornamental headpiece. Then he tore the rigging from the mast, bound the young ladies by the body to the slight rail-around the deck; cut away the mast; and, rising up in the water, waved his arm toward the shore.

At that signal the crowd shouted, and began to pull. The disabled craft obeyed the rope. Rolling, tossing, rising, falling, groaning, creaking in all its timbers, it approached the shore.

But the danger was coming. Within twenty yards of land an enormous wave rushed at the prey about to escape, and with one blow broke the frail craft into a dozen pieces.

The young ladies disappeared, and a great wave rolled over them.

Then they reappeared as suddenly. With his hatchet Earle cut the ropes which secured them to the pieces of wreck; the man of the boat seized one, and Earle seized the other;

five minutes afterwards, the fishermen had rescued the former; and then Earle appeared,
staggering, panting, struggling to reach dry
ground, the inanimate form of a girl clasped in
his arms.

The fishermen hastened tòward him.   A
great wave hurled itself — the last defiance of
the sea — in their faces, and forced them back.
But that wave drove Earle onward.

As it receded, he was on firm earth.

With his left arm around the girl, he raised
his right aloft as though waving his hat,
uttered a low cry of triumph, and, staggering,
fell upon the sand, his head upon the bosom of
the girl.

CHAPTER X.

HOW THE SAILOR EARLE BECAME ONE OF THE "WOLVES."

IN the afternoon of the same day, Earle was about to issue from the hostelry of the *Cat and Bell*, when a thundering knock at his door made him turn quickly toward a brace of pistols lying upon the table.

"Has my good friend Sir Murdaugh Westbrooke perchance gained an inkling of my real character, and of what is in store for him?" he muttered. And turning to the door,—

"Come in!" he said.

As he uttered the words, he cocked one of his pistols, prepared for whatever was to come.

The door opened, and the huge "wolf" with whom he had fought in the morning, entered.

IIis head nearly touched the low ceiling. His countenance was a great mass of shaggy hair. Low down on his forehead grew a similar mass, and he resembled rather a wild animal than a human being.

"I be come to see you, master," said the wolf.

"And who are you?" retorted Earle.

"My name be Goliath, master," returned the Anak, "and the wolves are waiting to catch you up and make you one of us."

Earle gazed at the speaker, and saw that this man was a friend. If there was any doubt of the fact, his next words removed it.

"I felt your hand to-day, master," said Goliath: "it is heavy, but I want to feel it again."

As he spoke, Goliath extended a paw as large nearly as a ham, and half covered with hair.

"Good!" said Earle; "there it is."

And he reached out his own. It was small, bronzed, and had the grasp of a vice.

The giant winced.

"It hits hard, and it hits fair," he said. "I be sorry I quarrelled, master; but I am going to make up that."

Suddenly he turned up Earle's cuff. A blue

anchor was tattooed, sailor-fashion, on the white wrist.

"I knew that," said Goliath; "nobody but a sailor would 'a' ventured as you did to-day."

"Well, I am a sailor."

"Which makes it all the better; you knocked me down, and after that I would 'a' fought you. You went out in the surf — and the 'longshore-men are a-going to make you a wolf!"

As he spoke a loud roar was heard in the street without, — evidently uttered by the wolves.

Earle laughed, and muttered, —

"A strange life this of mine! — to be made a chief of the Iroquois in Canada, and one of the wolves in Wales!"

The roar was again heard.

"The wolves be waiting, master!" said Goliath.

"Ready!" said Earle.

And walking beside the giant, he descended to the street, where a great crowd of tattered, fierce-looking and shaggy-bearded 'longshoremen were gathered with intent to do him honor.

"Stop your howling!" shouted Goliath, "and be orderly, will you!"

The roar ceased for a moment, but was resumed an instant afterwards with fresh zest. The noise seemed to excite the crowd. From hoarse shouts they proceeded to action. Earle suddenly found himself caught up, borne aloft in triumph, and then his captors at the head of whom was Goliath, surged into the low-pitched common-room of the inn, where Earle was placed upon a table in the midst.

At his side, on the floor stood Goliah, one hand on his shoulder.

"What be your name, master?" said the giant.

A singular sentiment moved the sailor. Content to assume a false name with indifferent persons or enemies, — with these rough friends it was different. Something uncontrollable within him made him answer, —

"Edmond Earle!"

At that reply a man who had been seated in a dark corner started, rose suddenly, and went out of the inn. As he disappeared, one of the 'longshoremen scowled after him and laid his hand on his knife. The man who had gone out was Wilde, the emissary of Sir Murdaugh Westbrooke; and Earle, in thus uttering his real name, had committed a terrible imprudence.

He did not see Wilde, however. The wolves

were admitting him, with rude ceremonies, into the pale of their order.

A gigantic beaker of usquebaugh was first raised to his lips; each drank from it in turn, and then the residue was poured upon the floor.

As the liquor fell from the beaker, Goliath exclaimed, in his voice of thunder, —

"So the blood of all who hunt the wolves shall be poured out!"

And clapping Earle on the shoulder, —

"From to-day you be a wolf, master!" he said.

The wolves roared in approbation.

"Join hands!" thundered Goliath.

At the word the wild figures linked hands and began to dance around the table. Earle had never witnessed so strange a spectacle. There was something at once ferocious and grotesque in these ragged figures circling the table in their mad dance. Three times they thus whirled around him, and then the circle broke and they again caught the sailor up on their shoulders. All resistance was impossible. He was borne forth and carried through the streets in triumph.

When, an hour afterwards, he was realeased,

and woke as it were from this orgy of dream-land, he saw Goliath standing beside him, and heard the giant say, —

"You be one of us now, master; and woe be to him who lays his hand on you!"

At the same moment the man Wilde entered Westbrooke Hall, and hastened to the baronet.

"Well?" said the master.

"I have something terrible to report, sir!" said the man.

"What?"

And the baronet rose, as if on steel springs.

"The person who visited you here last night, sir —"

Wilde paused.

"Speak!" shouted the baronet, shaking him by the collar.

"Is — who would have believed it —!"

The baronet's hand passed to the man's throat.

"Is — is —" muttered Wilde, in a half-strangled voice — "Edmond — Earle!"

The baronet turned ghastly pale, and stared at the speaker with stupefaction.

"Edmond — Earle!" he said in a low voice, "*the* Edmond Earle?"

"The same, sir. There was something familiar in his look."

The baronet's eyes blazed.

"Then he is not dead, after all!"

"No, since we have seen him sir, and I have heard him give his name as Earle."

In a few words the man related what had occurred at the inn.

"Yes — I see now — I was deceived," said the baronet in a low tone. "He is here — cool and determined — ready, and he knows my secret. Fool! — from this moment he is dead! Dead men tell no tales."

CHAPTER XI.

ELLINOR MAVERICK.

WHEN broken in upon by the wolves, Earle had been preparing to take a ride.

An hour after the ending of the ceremony which inducted him into the band of "wolves," he mounted a horse procured at the inn, and set out on his ride.

As he went on, a singular emotion agitated him. The occasion of this was the name of the gentleman and ladies whom he had rescued. This name was Maverick.

Maverick! Could it then be the head of this family whom Sir Murdaugh Westbrooke had murdered? Had no steps been taken to discover the criminal? Into what black mystery was he, Edmond Earle, about to plunge? He

had received the warm thanks of the gentleman
and two young ladies whom he had rescued.
They had urged "Mr. Delamere," in the most
pressing manner, to visit them at their home,
"Maverick House." The road had been
pointed out to the sailor; and, emerging from
the fishing village, he already saw the mansion
on its lofty hill, about a league distant.

He soon reached the great gate, and riding up
an avenue, dismounted and gave his bridle to a
servant. Maverick House was ancient, but
cheerful and inviting. Dogs were basking in
the sunshine on the long portico, where the light
filtrating through variegated foliage threw its
twinkling shadows; and on the steps stood,
smiling cordially and ready to welcome Earle, the
gentleman of the boat, Arthur Maverick.

Arthur Maverick was a young man of about
Earle's age; thin, pale, and sad-looking, but
courteous and cordial. He welcomed the sailor
warmly, and conducted him into the mansion,
whose appointments were at once substantial and
elegant. In a cage a linnet was singing; old
dogs wandered about; and a lapdog, small and
hideous, which made him immensely valuable,
ran yelping to announce the visitor to the two
young ladies whose lives he had saved.

Ellinor Maverick, the eldest, was tall, with raven hair and dark eyes, instinct with a subtle fascination. The great eyes melted or fired; the red lips, full and moist, curled satirically or were wreathed with dazzling smiles; in every outline of her rounded and supple figure there was the superb beauty of the animal — the tigress you were apt to think; and with only a slight effort of the imagination you might fancy the beautiful creature " in act to spring."

Rose Maverick was altogether different. About nineteen,—Ellinor was older,—slender, brown-haired, with soft, violet eyes, and an exquisite expression of candor and goodness, Rose made children and old ladies love her, and men take no notice of her. The latter went crazy about Ellinor, and did not even look at Rose. One was the dazzling sunlight, the other the pensive moonlight. From the first moment Earle's eyes were dazzled; and on his return to the inn that night, a strange throbbing of the heart accompanied his recollection of the superb Ellinor.

On the next day he went to Maverick House again, and on the next, and the next.

He was fascinated. That term best expresses his sentiment towards Ellinor Maverick. It would be incorrect to say that he *loved* her; he was crazy about her, and the great melting or blazing eyes had wrought the charm.

At times his neglect of the important object which had brought him to the coast of Pembrokeshire weighed heavily upon his spirits. Was he not criminally disobeying the orders which he had received? Was he not neglecting his sworn duty? Would not the crew of the corvette wonder what had become of their captain, and the boat at the secret rendezvous return nightly to find him still absent, paying no attention to his appointment? Earle asked himself those questions, and gloomily shook his head. Then he would find himself beside Ellinor Maverick. All his depression would disappear. Her golden smile would shine upon him, and the dazzled moth would circle careless around the light, drawing every moment nearer to his fate.

It came at last. Nearly ten days had elapsed since his first meeting with the young lady. He had never spoken of his love in plain words, for an instant, but now a little incident drove him to that proceeding.

Sir Murdaugh Westbrooke was the occasion of the denouement. Earle had well-nigh for-

gotten the baronet, and the strange history re-
lared by the gypsy. Was the "Giles Maverick,
Esquire," assassinated at the pool by him, a relative of the family at Maverick House? He
had intended, often, to ask that question, but
something had always prevented. Either the
occasion was wanting, or his interviews with
Arthur Maverick had been interrupted; always
something had intervened to withhold him from
ascertaining the truth.

At last the opportunity came. He was conversing with Arthur Maverick one evening,
when the latter pronounced the name of Sir
Murdaugh Westbrooke.

Earle looked keenly at him.

"Are you acquainted with that gentleman?"
he said.

"Very well," was the young man's reply.

"And he is a friend?"

Arther hesitated.

"No," he said, at length.

Earle observed a singular coldness in his companion's tones, and said, —

"You do not like the baronet?"

"I feel some delicacy in replying to that
question," returned Arthur Maverick.

"Why?" said Earle.

"Sir Murdaugh Westbrooke is a suitor for the hand of my cousin."

Earle started, and looked at his companion in utter astonishment.

"Your *cousin?* Sir Murdaugh her suitor? Who is your cousin, my dear Mr. Maverick?"

"Ellinor. I thought you knew that she was not my sister, Mr. Delamere. She is the daughter of my father's brother. On the death of that gentleman she had no home, and came to live with us here. You seem astonished."

"No, no," stammered Earle. "Sir Murdaugh Westbrooke a suitor! and for the hand of — why, 'tis monstrous!" And his face flushed. "That is to say — may I ask you a question, Mr. Maverick? You speak of your father's brother; he is dead, you say. Your father also is dead, is he not?"

"Some years since," was the reply, in a low tone.

"May I ask the cause of his death?"

Arthur Maverick's head sank.

"He was cruelly murdered, Mr. Delamere; and in the most mysterious manner!"

"Ah! a *murder*, sir!"

"An infamous murder, by whom we have never discovered. He left home one evening on horseback, and his dog returned some hours afterwards without him. It was a very intelligent blood-hound; he is still living, old and almost blind; and he led the way to a pool in the woods, where my father's body was discovered."

Earle remained for some moments silent. Then he said, —

" And no clue has ever been discovered to the murder ? "

" None whatever. It is still wrapped in the profoundest mystery."

Earle nodded his head coolly, and said, —

" Pardon my intrusive questions, Mr. Maverick; I see they agitate you, and I regret them. To return to the worthy Sir Murdaugh Westbrooke, your cousin's suitor. Does she smile upon him ? "

" I am afraid so."

" You say that in the tone of one who regrets a thing," said Earle, whose heart suddenly sank. "Is it possible that the baronet, an aged and not agreeable person, I think, has succeeded in the role of a lover ? "

Arthur Maverick did not reply for an instant, then he said, —

" We are not wealthy, sir. Ellinor has

nothing; and Sir Murdaugh is a person of great possessions."

" Ah! and hence he succeeds! Miss Maverick barters her beauty against money. Pardon my rudeness, sir; I am a sailor, and speak without ceremony. Her preferred suitor! It is monstrous! It cannot be! I will know the truth!"

And leaving his companion abruptly, Earle went with pale face and glowing eyes toward Ellinor Maverick, who was standing near one of the great windows in the drawing-room.

Her golden smile said " Come! you have stayed away from me too long!" Her glance was magnetic, alluring, almost passionate, and seemed to pierce through him.

" Is Sir Murdaugh Westbrooke your suitor?" he said. " Answer that question plainly, I pray you."

Her silver laugh rang out.

" Yonder he comes; why not ask him?" she said, pointing through the window. " Strange that you and he have never met before, Mr. Delamere!"

CHAPTER XII.

FEW minutes afterwards Sir Murdaugh Westbrooke entered, clad as became his rank, and grinning in his most attractive manner.

At sight of Earle, however, he suddenly grew livid, and the grotesque grin was succeeded by a glance full of menace.

For an instant their hostile glances flashed and crossed like rapiers. Then Earle regained his coolness, continued to converse with Ellinor Maverick; and that young lady's handsome back was turned upon Sir Murdaugh.

The baronet's expression thereat grew venomous. His demeanor toward Earle was a mixture of apprehension and suppressed rage; but no one noticed it — certainly not the fair

Ellinor, who leaned forward, resting her rosy cheek upon her snowy hand, so as to exhibit the charms of an exquisitely rounded arm, and gazed at Earle with an air of deep and fascinated interest.

That expression, in the eyes of a beautiful woman, is dangerous. It had its full effect upon the sailor. He felt his heart beat, and the blood rushed to his cheeks. Through a sort of haze he seemed to see an angel, or a devil, he knew not which, whose eyes said to him, "You did right to take me away from that hideous satyr yonder. We are young. Love is the only true life. Love me, and I will love you, and be yours!"

When a commonplace question from Rose Maverick broke the spell, Earle seemed to fall suddenly from some fairy realm into the cold world again. He turned quickly. Sir Murdaugh Westbrooke was looking at him and Ellinor with all the furies raging in his heart.

He rose — his visit had lasted less than an hour, but it had seemed a century of torment. Declaring stiffly that he had only ridden out to take the air, and must now return, he bowed low, shot a wrathful glance at Ellinor Maverick and went out, accompanied by Arthur Maverick, whose manner throughout the interview had been perfectly courteous but also perfectly formal.

Two hours afterwards, Earle in his turn mounted and directed his way toward the village.

His head was turning, almost. A passionate scene had occurred between himself and the fair Ellinor on the portico. She had magnetized him, drawn him on, said " Come!" with her eyes, and when he poured out his passion, quietly laughed at him.

Ten minutes afterwards, he was riding away; as he went he muttered to himself, —

" So that folly ends, and the end is fortunate, perhaps. Earle the sailor is not to cast anchor yet — so much the better; the wind is fair, and there is fighting and sailing to do. Fighting? Come! I think there was some question of that once! I've been crazy, but am sane now; I was dreaming, but am awake! To work, laggard! and obey your orders. You came hither under orders, and you are shirking your duty. Your men await you nightly, yonder; act this night, and leave the accursed land where you've fallen into a woman's toils! Come! to work! Ah! Sir Murdaugh Westbrooke, my dear assassin and rival, beware! This very night I will lay a heavy hand upon you!"

He was passing, as he thus muttered, through a dark hollow in the hills.

"It is time, brother!" said a voice, "or he will lay his hand on *you!*"

And the speaker advanced from the shadow of a huge hemlock, beneath which he had been concealed.

It was the gypsy.

CHAPTER XIII.

THE MAN IN THE COACH.

EARLE, startled for an instant in spite of himself, by the apparition in his path, quickly regained his coolness, and drew rein to converse with his companion.

"You say —?" said Earle.

"That Sir Murdaugh Westbrooke is plotting to destroy you," said the gypsy. "I know it from hearing the thing with my ears, brother."

"Tell me all about it."

And dismounting, Earle threw his bridle over his arm, and walked on beside the gypsy.

"Well, I will do so, brother. Night is the time to talk; and I think the stars yonder are friendly to the brethren of the Rommanye Rye. Here is the way I discovered all. I had been to make a visit to Westbrooke Hall —"

"Not to converse with the baronet on *that business?*" interrupted Earl.

The gypsy smiled in a manner which displayed a double row of teeth.

"No, brother. To tell you the truth, I don't like the thought of going there on that errand. Some accident might happen to me; I might be set up in a chair, opposite that other grinning 'old gentleman,' in the grave-clothes!"

"I understand," said Earle.

"I had other business, and I succeeded in it, brother. I had made a little plot against the other wolf-hound. Some day, I said, I may have to visit Westbrooke Park. Then the hound will prove an ugly customer, and give the alarm. Better act in time, and pay my respects to his honor, the wolf-hound!"

"I understand," repeated Earle.

"So I went to see this good watch-dog in his kennel," continued the gypsy; "and to make my visit more acceptable, carried with me a piece of fresh meat. This I threw to our friend, the hound, just as he sprung out to give the alarm. He gobbled it up instead of barking. I hid in the bushes near, and in about fifteen minutes the dog seemed to grow sick. Then he bit the ground and tugged at his chain, and ended by rolling on his back, beating the air with his paws, and then lying quiet." ·

"Poisoned?"

"Yes, brother. He is not apt to trouble us further. I saw that he was done for and hastened to retreat from the park. When I reached the great woods, I thought I was safe; but as I was gliding through a thicket skirting the main road, I thought I heard footsteps in the undergrowth, and lay down listening. The steps came nearer. From my covert I saw a man, with a gun on his shoulder, pass within twenty feet of me, and as he approached the road I could hear the hoof-strokes of a horse."

"The baronet?"

"Yes. He was coming back, it seemed, from a visit, as I soon found that he was in full dress. The man who was his gamekeeper, Wilde, had chanced to be going his rounds and met him. The baronet stopped, and I could see, through an opening, by the starlight, that his face was pale and full of anger at something."

Earle nodded.

"I can explain that. Well, you saw,— doubtless you also heard."

" Yes, brother, I was born with a great hank-ering after finding out everything. I crawled along, without making a noise, until I was within a few yards of these good people, and hiding in a clump of bush, listened. I had torn my rags to worse rags, but what I heard was worth the expense. I need not tell you what they said; it amounted to this — that you were to be waylaid and ' got rid of.' That was the baronet's phrase. As to me, I was to be treated in the same way. You see he knows *we know* his secret, and as long as we are alive he is not safe. He is in a violent rage with you at something, besides, which occurred to-night, it seems ; and, hearing the name, ' Maverick House,' where, it appears, you were on a visit, I thought I'd warn you in time, brother."

" You did well, — forewarned, forearmed," said Earle. " Was anything more said between the worthies ? "

"They were interrupted."

" By whom ? "

" As they were talking in low tones, on the side of the road, within a few feet of me, a fine coach, drawn by four horses, came along, going toward the Hall, and, as it passed, a gentleman put his head out of the window, and said, ' Is not that Sir Murdaugh Westbrooke ? ' — ' Yes,' the baronet replied. — ' I am the Viscount Cecil,' said the man in the coach.   And the baronet bowed, came up, talked for some minutes, and at last got into the coach, which rolled away toward the Hall, Wilde having taken his master's horse.   Then I set off to find you ; the grass has not grown under my feet.   What will you do, brother ? "

But Earle did not reply.   A sudden glow had come to his countenance.

" Are you sure you heard aright ? " he exclaimed.   " The man in the coach gave his name as Viscount Cecil ? "

" I heard the name distinctly, brother.   It seems to interest you."

" It does, I swear to you ! And you heard nothing more ? "

" Only something about his having come down to his estates, from Parliament, to see the baronet on business, or something of the sort."

" Good !   ' Parliament,' — that is enough ! ' Viscount Cecil,' — there can be no doubt.   It is he ! "

" What do you say, brother ? "

"Nothing. Ah, the man in the coach — the man in the coach! That decides me. I might have been weak — this makes me resolute!"

And turning to the gypsy, he added, —

"I am about to leave this country, brother. Do not count on my co-operation with you, and look out for yourself. One thing only I can promise you : I think that I will rid you of your enemy, Sir Murdaugh Westbrooke. All is ready! To-night decides! Farewell, brother! May the stars guide you!"

He uttered the last words in the gypsy tongue, and made a salute peculiar to the fraternity.

Then, putting spurs to his horse, he disappeared at full gallop in the darkness.

The gypsy gazed after him with an expression of wonder, and then began running in the same direction; that is, toward Oldport.

The village was not, however, Earle's destination now. Once out of sight of the gypsy, an individual whom he seemed to decline trusting, he turned to the right, rode rapidly toward the coast, reached the foot of the great headland, on which we have witnessed his interview with the sad-looking woman, and, dismounting, concealed his horse in a thicket.

He then advanced upon foot, without losing a moment, toward the spot where he had disembarked from the boat, and following a winding path, along narrow ledges of rock, came in sight of the little indentation in the precipice.

The boat was awaiting him. There were four men in it—they seemed to have just arrived.

CHAPTER XIV.

THE NIGHT MARCH, AND ITS OBJECT.

THE young sailor passed along the narrow ledge, with the activity of a chamois, and suddenly stood in presence of the boat's crew.

All hands went to their hats.

"Welcome, Captain!" said one whose tone was that of an officer; "you see we obey orders. I was growing uneasy."

"Thanks, Dargonne! Well, the time has arrived. The affair will take place to-night. Come ashore, order the men to follow us. I see they are armed, as I ordered. Direct them to make no noise and come on quickly, keeping us in sight."

Lieutenant Dargonne, a small wiry-looking

personage, clad in plain clothes, like the men, turned and communicated Earle's orders.

The men silently stepped from the boat: attached it to a splintered rock by a chain, and followed Earle and Dargonne, who passed back along the narrow path by which Earle had come.

Reaching the slope of the headland again toward the interior, Earle went to the thicket in which he had tethered his horse, untied the animal, led him by the bridle, and, followed by the sailors, made a circuit so as to avoid Oldport, and approached Westbrooke Hall.

"The moment has come now, my dear Dargonne," he said to his companion, "to tell you my project. I have not done so before, in obedience to orders. A few words will explain everything. France and England are at war. In America the war has been barbarous, they say, on the part of England, and it seems growing as barbarous here. The English admiralty have issued orders to their cruisers to descend upon the French coast, whenever an opportunity offered, and carry off persons of position and influence to be held as hostages. This policy has been adopted in obedience to the wishes of the English party in power, and this party is

led in Parliament by Viscount Cecil, who made
a violent oration urging the policy I speak of.
His oration was reported in the English journals;
— these were transmitted to His Majesty, King
Louis; in consequence, the cruisers of His
Majesty have received orders to retort by de-
scending upon the English coast and carrying
off any persons of rank and importance whom
they can lay their hands on."

Dargonne made a sign that he understood
perfectly.

"Blow for blow! That is only fair," he
said.

"Entirely fair, my dear Dargonne; and now
to come to the work before us. When I received the general order to land at any point I
thought proper on the English coast for the
object in view, I decided to visit the coast of
Pembrokshire, hoping to seize the Viscount
Cecil himself. I had already visited this coast,
as you know; and the viscount's large estates
lay near Oldport. I might find him at home
after Parliament, and that would be superb.
So I came, but soon found that the viscount
was still in London; then I planned the seizure
of a cousin of his, Sir Murdaugh Westbrooke.
I visited Westbrooke Hall to reconnoitre, and

did so. Then the attack would have been made — it should have been — but I have been weak, Dargonne! No more of that — it is over! I am Earle the sailor again, and will act like him. I was to have made my attack on Westbrooke Hall to-night, my object being to carry off the baronet, the viscount's cousin. But suddenly an immense piece of good fortune has happened to us. The viscount himself has arrived!"

"Viscount Cecil?"

"Himself — to-night."

"The man who set the whole policy against France in motion!"

"The very man. And think — we shall seize him to-night! He is at Westbrooke Hall!"

Dargonne clucked his tongue in a rapturous manner.

"Magnificent!" he exclaimed.

"Is it not?" said Earle, his eyes sparkling with joy. "Such an opportunity to win rank and distinction is seldom offered to a privateersman."

"Not in one hundred years, Captain! It is splendid — unheard of. Viscount Cecil — not only a Lord, but the man His Majesty hates! We will be presented — thanked, at court. Jean Bart will be forgotten!"

Earle made a gesture checking his companion.

"The work is not done; we may fail," he said.

"Fail?"

"May not succeed in seizing his lordship and the baronet, for I aim to secure both. All human affairs are doubtful."

"This *must* succeed! What are the obstacles? Are there retainers to meet our cutlasses — dogs to alarm them?"

"Fortunately no dogs. The only one was poisoned to-night and will not be able to announce our approach. And as to retainers, they are few. The viscount, and possibly the baronet, will, however, make resistance."

"A trifle."

"Let us undervalue nothing, Dargonne. I have succeeded and failed; but if I fail now, it will be after exhausting every effort. The viscount is at Westbrooke Hall — there it is through the opening in the trees yonder! We will approach without noise, and enter either by surprise or escalade. If the viscount is captured, he will be mounted on this horse — the baronet on another from his own stables, — and they will be conducted rapidly to the boat, thence to the corvette; and we will make sail for France, and be out of sight of the coast by daylight."

They had reached the wall of the park. Earle threw the bridle of his horse over a bough in a sheltered nook, and at one bound cleared the wall, followed by Dargonne and the sailors.

As he did so, a shadow glided from beneath an oak. At one bound Earle seized the shadow —it was the gypsy.

"You hurt my throat, brother," said the gypsy.

"Ah, it is you! How did you come here?"

"I followed you, brother," returned the vagabond coolly; "and if you are willing, I will help you in your work."

Earle reflected for an instant. It was plain that the gypsy had no motive to prove false to him; and the presence of the men made it impossible for him to escape and give the alarm if he wished to do so.

"It is well, brother," said Earle; "follow me and obey my directions."

The gypsy fell back to the ranks of the sailors.

"See that the men make no noise now, Dargonne," said Earle, "and above all, that no fire-arms are used. The attack will be made from the rear of the house, to prevent resistance and an alarm. Let every one preserve silence and follow me."

As he spoke, they came to the desolate-looking expanse immediately in front of Westbrooke Hall.

CHAPTER XV.

THE VISCOUNT CECIL.

ET us precede the assaulting party, and ascertain what was going on in Westbrooke Hall at the moment when they silently followed the path through the woods to seize the coveted prize.

In the large apartment where the interview between Earle and the baronet had taken place, Sir Murdaugh Westbrooke and the Viscount Cecil were seated, coldly conversing.

The viscount was a gentleman of commanding appearance, and had once been handsome; ill health, or some other cause, however, had reduced a frame once powerful. It was an invalid, almost, who talked with the baronet, but an invalid of superb and commanding expression and bearing.

"I have long desired to hold this interview, but have been constantly prevented, sir," he said to the baronet, in a cold tone.

"Its object, my lord?" was the formal question of the baronet.

"Family affairs; and to propose to you an arrangement which may prove agreeable to us both."

Sir Murdaugh Westbrooke became more formal and stiff than before. Two icebergs seemed to have encountered each other; under the frozen crust of these men's countenances no emotion of any description was discernible.

"An 'arrangement,' my lord?—you have an arrangement to propose to me?" said the baronet, with ill-concealed suspicion. "I listen, and shall be glad to know of what character it is."

The Viscount remained for a moment silent, his eyes fixed upon the floor; then he raised his head and said in measured and formal tones,—

"Permit me, in the first place, to state briefly the relations we now sustain toward each other, sir. That will lead to a clear understanding of the offer I propose to make you. When the last Lord Wentworth died, he was almost without blood relations. Two young cousins, you and myself, sir, were the nearest, and were selected by him to be his heirs. By his will, you were to have the great Westbrooke property here; I that upon which his lordship had resided in this neighborhood. That is correct, is it not, sir?"

"Wholly correct, my lord," was the cold reply.

"I will proceed, then, sir. There was a proviso in the will, that if either you or myself died without issue, the survivor should inherit. Thus the entire property of Lord Wentworth would remain in his family. That also is correct, sir, is it not?"

"Entirely, my lord."

"Well, now for my proposition, sir. I do not propose to marry, and think it improbable that you design doing so. Thus you will inherit from me, or I will inherit from you: the chance is even, perhaps. I am an invalid, but one of those invalids who live longer than strong men; and your age is greater by some years than mine — in brief, I may survive you."

"It is possible, as your lordship says," returned the baronet, with his ghastly grin.

"Well, I propose a compromise; and I will

be entirely frank, sir, in stating its object. A great grief has rendered me lonely,— the death of my wife,— a fact of which you are aware. I am solitary and crave affection; thus I have fixed my regards upon a young lady whom I wish to adopt as my daughter. To this young lady I wish to leave a portion of my property; in fine, I propose, sir, to convey to you, now, one-half my entire estate, if, in return, you will execute an instrument settling the other half on the young lady, to be her own at my death."

"The name of the young lady, my lord, if you please?" said Sir Murdaugh, coldly.

"It is unimportant — I will withhold it for the present. What say you to my proposition, sir?"

Sir Murdaugh Westbrooke rose, with a grin of unconcealed triumph.

"I say that circumstances render it impossible for me to accept it, my lord!"

"Circumstances? Of what nature, sir?"

"I will be franker than your lordship. The circumstance of my approaching marriage."

"*Your* marriage?"

"Your lordship dwells upon the word 'your;' it is scarce polite."

The viscount suddenly grew freezing.

"Your pardon, sir. It was, indeed, scant courtesy. I will not further trouble you, save to congratulate you upon your approaching nuptials."

The baronet bowed ironically.

"I can understand, sir," said the viscount, in the same tone, "that your parental anticipations quite overturn my own views. Your children may inherit my estate: so be it, sir. God has so decreed it."

Something like a convulsion passed over the pale face. Then it resumed its expression of lofty and commanding calmness, and the viscount said,—

"Will you be good enough to order my coach, sir? I will sleep at my own home to-night."

As he uttered the words, the window in the adjoining room was driven in by a heavy blow, the sash was thrown up, and Earle, at the head of his men, leaped into the apartment.

CHAPTER XVI.

THE ATTACK AND PURSUIT.

ARLE advanced with drawn sword toward the viscount and baronet.

"Surrender, or you are dead!" he said, presenting the point to the viscount's heart.

The nobleman's reply was to draw his dress-sword, and lunge straight at Earle's breast.

But the sailor was far too powerful for him. With a whirl of his weapon, he sent the dress-sword of the viscount spinning across the room.

In spite of his disarmed condition, the viscount continued to resist, and was with difficulty secured.

"No harm is designed your lordship," said Earle.

And he wheeled round to seize Sir Murdaugh Westbrooke.

The baronet had disappeared, the explanation of which was simple.

Sir Murdaugh Westbrooke, for reasons best known to himself, had amused his leisure moments by constructing in the wall of the apartment a secret door, which opened by means of a spring and closed in the same manner. Was the secret recess, or means of exit, intended to be employed in the event of a sudden advance by the officers of the law upon him? It is impossible to say, but there was the means of safety at hand, and the baronet made use of it.

Finding that the viscount was in the power of the midnight assailants, Sir Murdaugh Westbrooke determined to save himself. At one bound he reached the wall, leaned against the concealed knob, the door flew open, the baronet passed through it, and the panel flew to again, protecting, with its three inches of solid oak, the fugitive from all further danger.

Thus the baronet had evaded him, but Earle had secured the greater prize. The frightened servants had fled at the first noise, and no opposition was made.

"Now to gain the boat," said Earle; "no

time is to be lost, as the alarm may be given ! ”

He made a sign and the great front door was thrown open.

“Your lordship will please go with us quietly,” he said to the nobleman.

And the party, with the viscount in charge, passed out and hurried through the park. They soon reached the spot where they had entered, found the horse quietly awaiting them; and Earle, with perfect courtesy, requested the viscount to mount. He did so without uttering a word. One of the sailors led the animal by the bridle; Earle and Dargonue walked on each side. The rest followed, and the cortege set out rapidly in the direction of the coast.

When they had gone a hundred yards, Earle turned to the viscount and said, —

“I beg that your lordship will have no apprehensions. No harm will be done you, if you make no resistance.”

“Very well, sir ” was the viscount’s reply, in a cold and unmoved voice; “that at least is gratifying. You have not asked for my purse, I observe.”

Earle colored with anger, but suppressed this emotion at once.

" We do not wish to inspect the contents of your lordship's pockets," he said, stiffly.

" May I ask your object, then, sir, in committing this extraordinary outrage upon my person ? "

" The object was to capture your lordship," said Earle calmly.

" To capture me ? "

" Precisely."

" For what reason ? I am really curious to ascertain the object which you have in view, sir. You appear to be a person of good breeding, if I may judge of your character by the tones of your voice ; and I need not inform you that curiosity is most painful when left ungratified."

There was a coolness and nonchalance in the viscount's tones which highly pleased Earle, and made him respect his adversary.

" I compliment your lordship on your calmness, and thank you for your good opinion The object of this little night attack need not remain a secret. It is now unimportant whether your lordship knows or is ignorant of the meaning of every thing. We shall carry you off, — it is probable at least, — and I trust that the safety of my men will not require me to put your lordship to death. I should regret that, and will not contemplate so painful a catastrophe."

"You turn your sentences charmingly, sir; and now for your object in carrying me off?"

"It is my design to conduct you to France, my lord."

"To France?"

"To the court of his French majesty."

"A prisoner?"

"Of state or war, as you choose."

"Ah! I begin to understand. You retaliate for the late order of the English admiralty against French civilians!"

"Precisely, my lord."

"Then this affair assumes quite another aspect. Your name and rank?—you are a French officer?"

"I am, my lord. I have assumed the name of Delamere, but I am a captain in His Majesty's navy, and my true name is Edmond Earle."

The viscount bowed.

"All this changes things greatly, and no blame whatever attaches to you, sir," he said coldly. "I regarded you, very naturally, as a bandit bent on plunder. I beg you to pardon that injustice, since you are an officer acting in obedience to orders. Thanks for the information thus communicated. I do not care to know anything further."

And the viscount relapsed into silence, busy, it seemed, with his own thoughts.

Earle said no more, and the party proceeded rapidly on their way. Following the road by which they had come, they made the circuit of Oldport; and then Earle hastened still more, expecting every moment to hear or see something that would give the alarm. Sir Murdaugh's first thought after the disappearance of the assailants would undoubtedly be to arouse the country — the audacious party might be followed, and either captured or killed; all depended now upon expedition; and Earle pressed on at the head of his men toward the spot where the boat had been left.

Suddenly the beacon light on the headland shot up, and threw its ruddy glare around.

"What is that, pray?" said the viscount, coolly.

"A misfortune, my lord," said Earle; "at least to us, for it will dissipate the darkness."

And glancing at the beacon fire he muttered, —

" Why is that kindled to-night ? "

He looked up. The appearance of the heavens explained all. Across the sky drifted rapidly black masses of cloud ; and the hoarse roar from the channel indicated that a storm was approaching. Doubtless the solitary had seen that, and kindled her beacon to warn vessels off the headland.

Earle's brows were knit, and he hurried on.

All at once, from an elevated point on the coast south of Oldport, a piece of artillery sent its long, hoarse thunder on the air.

" There is the alarm, my lord," said Earle. " Sir Murdaugh has not spared horseflesh and, the revenue station has given the alarm."

" Do you think there is a probability of my rescue, sir ? " said the viscount, with great coolness.

" None at all, I am pleased to say, my lord."

" I will pay each one who takes part in rescuing me, a thousand guineas," said the viscount, looking at the sailors.

Earle laid his hand on his pistol and frowned.

" Will your lordship be good enough to

forbear from further observations of that nature?" he said, sternly, "If my men are tempted again, I will blow out your brains, my lord!"

The Viscount inclined his head, with unmoved coolness.

"You are right" he said; "it was an indiscretion under the circumstances! I will therefore say no more, but await events."

"You will do well, my lord. You will now dismount, if you please. We are near the spot where a boat awaits you.'

The viscount dismounted without objection.

Earle then hastened at the head of his party toward the narrow path along the ledge of rocks, leading to the spot where the boat was awaiting him.

All at once the noise of hoofs was heard in the direction of Oldport. Lights danced to and fro. The gun had given the alarm.

"What noise, pray, is that?" said the viscount, quietly.

"The mounted guard of the revenue station — they have ridden well, and seem to be piloted by some one!"

"The affair grows interesting!" said the viscount, walking calmly beside Earle.

'I think we'll get off with your lordship!"
was the cool reply. And turning round,—

"Lose not a moment!" he said to the men;
" the cavalry are on us!"

The sudden smiting of hoofs within two
hundred yards came like an echo.

" To the ledge of rocks!" cried Earle; "once
there we are nearly safe!"

The hoof-strokes were silent.

" Quick! they are dismounting!" cried Earle.

All at once the pursuers were seen passing
around a clump of bushes. They were following on foot — about ten men under an officer,
and the gigantic plume of fire on the headland
showed them their game.

Earle knit his brows savagely.

" We will reach the boat or die fighting!"
he said. " Come, my lord!"

And he dragged the viscount on.

" There is, then some hope of my escape?"
said the latter, coolly.

" None!" was Earle's stern reply. " I shall
probably have the great honor of — dying with
with your lordship!"

CHAPTER XVII.

GOLIATH.

THE sailor had scarcely uttered these words when a sudden darkness spread itself over the landscape.

The beacon fire disappeared as though a tempest had extinguished it. Had the wind blown it out, or had the recluse heaped fresh wood upon it in such quantities as to temporarily smother the blaze? It was impossible to say, but the light suddenly disappeared. Earle and his party were completly concealed from his pursuers.

The sailor uttered an exclamation of triumph.

"We are saved if the darkness continues!" he said.

"The beacon seems extinguished, sir," said the voice of the viscount in the darkness.

"Yes, my lord?"

"What does it mean?'

"Fresh wood or the wind, probably."

"That is unfortunate."

"Or fortunate."

"You are right, sir. We look at things, very naturally, in a different light. This path is extremely narrow."

"Your lordship runs no danger, holding my arm. Come! our pursuers are nearly upon us!"

"The revenue guard?"

"Yes, my lord."

"They are pressing you close, captain. Is it your intention, if I may ask, to blow out my brains rather than lose me? I ask from mere curiosity; only to know what is coming."

"You are a brave man!" was Earle's reply. "No! a thousand times no! I am ordered to seize you, not to murder you!"

The viscount nodded.

"You say I am brave—I say that you are an officer and a gentleman. Now I will await the sequel. I have little further solicitude."

"And yet you are in very great danger."

"What?"

"Your friends may fire on us, and kill you!"

As Earle uttered the words a voice cried "Halt!" and a shot was heard.

The sailor staggered.

"You are struck!" exclaimed the viscount.

"Yes, my lord — and badly hurt, I think. But no matter!"

"I swear I regret it!"

"Thanks!"

"Surrender! I give you my word of honor you shall be treated as an officer captured on honorable duty."

"Surrender? never!" gasped Earle; "I will die fighting before I will surrender!"

And clutching the arm of the viscount, he dragged him violently toward the boat.

The pursuers were rushing upon them with loud shouts. The darkness hid them, but the noise of their footsteps on the rocky ledge betrayed them.

Earle dragged the viscount on. They reached the boat.

"Make haste! make haste, Dargonne! Every instant counts!" cried Earle.

And pushing the viscount without ceremony, —

"Enter the boat, my lord," he said, sternly.

" Then I am not to be rescued after all, it seems," was the philosophic reply of the viscount as he stepped upon the boat.

The men leaped after him and Dargonne followed.

" Come, Captain !" shouted Dargonne.

As he spoke, the foremost pursuers rushed on Earle. He felt a hand upon his throat. Then something like a heavy thump was heard in the darkness, and the man who had seized Earle was hurled back as by the blow of a bludgeon.

A second dull thump followed, and a second was prostrated in the same manner.

Earle staggered to the boat which had not moved.

" Put off, and return for me !" he exclaimed.

" Never !" Dargonne cried.

" Obey !" said Earle, imperiously. " It is I who give orders here !"

Dargonne bowed his head. Discipline conquered. He made a sign, and the boat flew a dozen yards from shore.

" Row, row !" cried Earle; " they are about to fire on you !"

A volley came like an echo, and one of the oarsmen uttered a cry of pain.

"Row!" cried Earle a second time; and the boat darted toward the open sea.

The sailor turned then to face his enemies, resolved to die as he had promised he would. But suddenly a voice near him said,—

"I have knocked down the foremost! Run up yonder and you be safe, master!"

It was the voice of Goliath, the "wolf."

"You?" said Earle.

"I came ahead, thinking it was smugglers, meaning to fight for 'em, master. It be you, which is better. You be a 'wolf.' There is the path."

He spoke hurriedly and pointed to the path leading up the cliff. Suddenly, shouts close at hand indicated that the main body of the pursuers had reached the spot. Earle had just time to rush behind a rock and up the path when the ledge swarmed with his enemies.

He hastened on up the steep path. His wound was bleeding profusely, and already his strength was nearly exhausted.

He tore open the bosom of his shirt, and bound up the wound in the best manner possible. But the linen was almost instantly saturated with blood.

Earle staggered on.

His head began to turn, and more than once he came near falling.

Still he continued the painful ascent: the strength of his powerful will alone seemed to sustain him.

At length, he had nearly reached the summit, where stood the hut of the recluse. The path wound around a ledge jutting over the sea.

As Earle tottered along this path, on the very edge of the dizzy precipice, the beacon fire shot aloft suddenly — a great pillar of flame.

Earle looked seaward. Half a mile from the headland, the boat containing the viscount was seen rapidly making for the open channel.

"Safe!" the sailor muttered, "they will soon reach the corvette."

And he tottered on up the broken pathway, his bosom heaving, his sight failing him.

A few more steps, and he reached the summit. Before him was the beacon and the hut. The solitary woman was seated on her bench.

Earle staggered toward her.

"Mother!" came from him in a low murmur.

A moment afterwards he had fallen, lifeless, nearly, upon the bosom of his mother.

PART II.

THE BLOOD-HOUND.

CHAPTER I.

HUNTED.

SINCE the events just related more than a month had passed.

Sir Murdaugh Westbrooke was seated in his library at Westbrooke Hall — cold, grim, gloomy, and knitting his brows, under which rolled, in their cavernous sockets, the threatening and bloodshot eyes.

"To think that he should have escaped!" he muttered; "and some day he will reappear — I feel it — and destroy me by uttering one word. What devilish accident ever threw him with

(118)

that gypsy whom I have been hunting in vain? That vagabond, no doubt, witnessed *what took place yonder*, while prowling in the woods."

He half shuddered.

"I am standing on a volcano!" he added in the same hoarse growl. "At any instant I may be destroyed. Not by the gypsy: no one would credit the statement of a worthless vagrant against Sir Murdaugh Westbrooke; but *he — his* statement — that is different. *He* is bold, determined; a man of character, and can ruin me if he chooses. He will return hither; that girl has made him her slave. Oh! to find him! to drive a bullet through him! to seal his lips by pistol or poniard, and at one blow insure my safety, and what is almost as important—!"

He turned round suddenly. Hurried steps were heard in the corridor. He started to his feet, turned pale, and his eye fell upon a brace of pistols lying on the table.

Wilde entered, or rather rushed in.

"You?"

The baronet drew a long breath.

"What is the matter?"

"Something important, your honor!" exclaimed the gamekeeper.

And in hurried words he explaimed the cause of his abrupt entrance. We shall sum up his communication in a few words. Knowing his master's anxiety to ascertain all in reference to Earle and the attack on the hall, he had exerted himself to the utmost in his character of spy and secret emissary. Lurking and listening at the *Cat and Bell*, and keeping his eyes as well as his ears open, he had managed on this day to ascertain the fact that Earle was wounded on the night of the attack. He had then examined the ground where the embarkation on the boat had taken place; observed the path up the precipice; ascended it; concealed himself behind a rock; seen Earle through the window of the hut, and hastened back to his master with this highly important intelligence.

It acted like a blow.

The baronet started to his feet, and exclaimed,—

"At last! this removes every danger at once!"

"He is a desperate man, sir," said Wilde. "We must take a party with us."

"Right. I'll send a note to the officer commanding at the revenue station."

And sitting down, he hurriedly wrote,—

"Sir,—Information has just reached me that the leader of the party who attacked my house some time since, and carried off the Viscount Cecil, is now lurking on the coast, at a point not far from Oldport.

"As the attack on my house was a personal grievance, and the abduction of my cousin, the Viscount Cecil, another, I offer to take command of a party to arrest the chief of the bandits. If you approve of this, send the men to Westbrooke Hall without delay. Loss of time will probably defeat the object in view."

This note he signed, sealed, and dispatched by Wilde himself.

Three hours afterwards the man returned, at the head of half a dozen mounted men. The shades of evening approached. It was the best hour for their project. Without a word, Sir Murdaugh Westbrooke mounted his horse, and made a sign to Wilde to do likewise. Then they set out, followed by the men, over nearly the same path which Earle and his party had pursued, which enabled them to avoid Oldport.

Wilde had made this suggestion.

"Better not pass through the village, sir," he said; "the wolves do not like you, from your activity in arresting their friends the smugglers. More than this — *he* is one of them. They made him a wolf in regular form a month or more ago. They will warn him or resist you; for they are capable of anything."

"You are right," returned Sir Murdaugh in a low tone; "lead the way by the safest road. There must be no failure — and listen, Wilde!"

He sunk his voice still lower.

"This man must not be arrested!"

Wilde returned the meaning glance.

"He must die!"

The man nodded.

"I understand you, sir; better give your orders."

The party were following a bridle-path through the woods. Sir Murdaugh West-brooke turned to the men.

"Let every man pay attention!"

All eyes were bent on him.

"The man we are in pursuit of is a desperate character. If he makes the least resistance, kill him. You will know if he resists by my firing upon him. At that signal, every man aim at his heart!"

The men were regular soldiers, and accustomed to obey orders without dispute. Their heads moved in assent; and, directing them to follow him at the distance of twenty yards, the baronet rode on with Wilde.

"This is better, after all," he said in a low tone, with a gloomy and lowering frown; "this man must die for more reasons than one. He knows what will destroy both you and me — he stands in my way yonder at Maverick House; and there is still another reason, as I need not tell *you*, which makes his death necessary."

He paused a moment, and added in a still lower tone.

"Let him die, then! And there is no reason to spare him. He is an enemy of the country, and has committed burglary and abduction. His life is forfeited to the law. He will hang for what he has done. But before he hangs he will speak, Wilde! — he will speak, do you hear? And then it is you and I who will mount the gallows after him."

Wilde's expression of countenance was one of much disgust at this announcement. The word "gallows" seemed to have a sickening effect upon him. He shuddered.

"Your honor is right. There is nothing to do but shoot him down. I have my carbine ready; and he will not get off."

"Good!"

And the baronet rode on in silence. The party made the circuit of Oldport, keeping in the shadow of the woods. Evening gradually drew near, and just at sunset they reached the forest on the slope of the headland, from which it was easy to gain on foot the path leading up the precipice.

"Dismount and follow me," said the baronet, addressing the men.

And they silently dismounted, tethered their horses, and followed the baronet and Wilde.

The gamekeeper rapidly led the way along the ledge to the spot where the boat had awaited Earle. They did not look out toward the channel upon which the mists of night had descended. Had they done so, they might have perceived a small boat vigorously rowing towards the headland; and on the horizon of water, a dusky sail beating up in the same direction.

Both escaped the attention of Wilde and the baronet.

"It was here that the viscount was brought," said Wilde, "and our man escaped up that path. Better tell the men to be quiet. I will lead the way, your honor."

"Do so."

He followed Wilde, and was followed in turn by the men.

As they ascended the steep and dangerous path, the last red beams of the sun died away in the channel mist; and the moon, a great crimson wheel, was rolled into the eastern sky above the fringe of the savage looking evergreens on the horizon.

" Did he go up this path after being wounded ? It is hard to believe that," muttered the baronet.

" There is the proof of it."

And Wilde pointed to blood-stains on a rock.

" He must have leaned against that rock ; and he went this way, or by some other, as I saw him yonder."

" Yes, yes ! Come, we are losing time !"

And he hastened after Wilde up the dangerous pathway.

" Who is this woman with whom he has taken refuge ?" he panted.

" A strange character ; a sort of solitary."

" I have heard of her."

" You will see her soon. There is the hut."

And Wilde pointed to the cabin of the recluse.

In a few minutes they had passed the dizzy ledge near the summit, and just as the last light of day was dying away from the headland, the baronet, at the head of Wilde and the men, rushed upon the hut.

In a moment they reached it, and the baronet, pistol in hand, threw himself against the door.

It yielded and flew open. The baronet raised his weapon.

But all at once his arm fell, and he staggered back as though a heavy blow had struck him. By the last light of day, it could be seen that his face had grown livid. Crouching, his mouth half open, and displaying in full relief the hideous tusks at each corner, with eyeballs starting from his head almost, and a cold sweat bursting forth upon his forehead, he was gazing at the solitary woman, who, erect, cold, and with her eyes fixed intently upon him, stood stiffly in the centre of the apartment.

"You!" exclaimed the baronet, in a voice nearly stifled by fear or astonishment. "You! Is it a corpse I see? You! Then you are not dead!"

"I am alive, as you see," returned the recluse, in a cold and unmoved voice.

Sir Murdaugh Westbrooke recoiled, gazing

at her with an air of stupefaction. In spite of his self-possession, he trembled.

"You!" he repeated. And he drew a long, deep breath, as though something were pressing heavily upon his breast.

"I, and I alone! He whom you seek is not here."

The baronet glanced around. It was utterly impossible that any one could be concealed in the cabin.

"Good!" he said. "That matter can wait, then. I see you know on what errand I came. I, in my turn, wish to know how it is that you are alive, and what brings *you* here?"

He turned to Wilde.

"Go with the men to their horses. I will soon rejoin you."

Wilde inclined his head, and went with the party in the direction indicated, only he took a path leading down the slope toward the interior, not that by which they had come.

"Now for much in a short space," said the baronet, looking sidewise at the woman.

It was an evil look, and his hand was on his pistol as he spoke.

"Neither of us know how long we may live," added the baronet, with a gastly grin; "and be fore we die it will be as well that we should have a short talk together, madam."

"I listen, Sir Murdaugh Westbrooke," said the recluse, seating herself composedly.

"Your manners remain as lofty as ever, I perceive, madam."

"It is natural, since I am Lady Westbrooke, sir."

"True, madam," came with an ominous scowl from the baronet, who remained standing. "I had lost sight of — or forgotten the fact that you are my wife."

CHAPTER II.

THE BARONET AND THE SOLITARY.

THE solitary woman gazed at him with perfect coolness and even with curiosity.

"You no doubt regret the fact that I am Lady Westbrooke, sir," she said; "but that is the truth, nevertheless. It affords me little gratification to claim the title, but I cannot discard it. We meet to-night for the first time for twenty years nearly; and a bad errand brings you hither. Better that you had not come — "

"And intruded myself upon your ladyship! Well, perhaps you are right; but I have little time at present. Answer me : how and when and why did you come to live in this wild spot ? '

"Many years since."

(129)

" Your object ? "

" To prevent you from committing a great sin."

" Thanks, madam, for your pious guardianship; but may I beg to be informed what sin you allude to ? "

" A second marriage during my life — the life of your lawful wife," was the calm response.

Sir Murdaugh Westbrooke's countenance assumed an expression utterly hideous at these words.

" Ah! that is the sin which you kindly propose to prevent me from committing, madam ? " he growled.

" It is."

" You are a hypocrite! You came hither with some other object ! " he half shouted.

This sudden rage brought a defiant flush to the solitary's pale face.

" You charge me with lying, then ? " she said, coldly.

" Yes : deception is your element."

" This to me, from you ! That is wonderful, sir, and well-nigh surpasses belief."

The words seemed to still further increase the rage of the baronet, and his glance grew terrible. More than once, a sudden clutch on the weapon in his grasp seemed to indicate a mad desire to remove then and there this obstacle from his path.

But his fury had no effect upon the woman: she remained cold and composed.

"Listen, Sir Murdaugh Westbrooke," she said. "You charge me with deceiving you, and coming hither with some covert and unworthy object. Do you think my past life — an unhappy life — supports that idea? What was that life, and what did you make it? I was a happy girl in the village of Martigny in Normandy, as gay as the roses blooming under our bright French sun, when one day there came to my father's house in the village, a young Englishman. Chance brought on this visit, and my wretched beauty — they said I was beautiful — did the rest. My father, an officer of the navy, was absent, and my old aunt watched over me. You were that young Englishman, sir. You won over my aunt; you became enamoured of me; you would have made me your victim, if I had not been too ignorant even to understand your base hints; and in the end, when you found that I was unassailable, you were mastered by your passion for me — you proposed for my hand, and my aunt forced me to marry you. The ceremony took place: I became Lady Westbrooke."

The baronet grinned hideously. The yellow teeth protruded like the tusks of a wild boar.

"You narrate with extreme clearness, madam, and recall the happy days of my life. Yes, I, an Englishman of rank, married the daughter of a poor sea-captain. He was lost at sea, nearly at the moment I married you. Thus you were a mere pauper, having nothing beside his pay. Well, what next, madam?"

The face of the solitary flushed hot.

"This it is to be a person of 'rank,' sir! You taunt a poor woman with her poverty — you hint that I was designing, sir. I loathed you at the very moment, when I placed my hand in yours; my aunt compelled me to marry you. French girls have no word in these arrangements. Yes, my poor father was dead — would he had appeared and forbidden the terrible sacrifice I was forced to make."

A sneer settled on the baronet's face.

"Well, all this is interesting, madam," he said, "but not very important. Oblige me by coming to the events which brought Lady Westbrooke to this crag on the coast of Wales."

"I will gratify your curiosity, sir," the recluse said, coldly, "and tell you everything without reservation. You had married me for my face merely, and six months afterwards were tired of the face. You began to treat me badly — wearied of the quiet of the old house in Martigny where we had lived since the day we were united. In the end you began to quarrel; you treated me cruelly, and laughed in my aunt's face, when she wished you to take me to your own house and acknowledge me publicly as Lady Westbrooke. That enraged my aunt; but *I* had a much greater ground for melancholy. You were a Protestant, I a Catholic. I had thus married a heretic, and the union, in my eyes, was sinful."

"Which led you, my dear madam, to desert me — "

"Just as you were on the point of deserting me. Yes, sir."

"Well, you are right, madam; I acknowledge that my married life had grown cursedly wearisome. I was thinking of leaving you and your doll face, and had even prepared to do so. It was a coincidence — two fond spouses mutually plotting in secret to desert each other."

The woman preserved a disdainful silence.

"Think! the affair was really comic!" added the baronet, grinning. "You watching me, and I watching you; each afraid that the other would discover the secret; each fearing detection, pursuit, and a renewal of the hateful union, while each in reality thirsted for the separation."

"Have you finished, sir?" said the recluse, coldly. "If so, I will continue."

"I have finished, madam," returned the baronet, with a bow of mock respect, "and shall be glad to hear the rest of your ladyship's interesting narrative."

"It shall be communicated in few words, sir. You were cruel to me; treated me with contempt; more than once were near striking me; in addition to which you were a heretic, and I was perilling my soul's salvation by listening in silence to your sneers at our holy church. Then I prayed for guidence from heaven, and something said to me, 'Leave him: he will destroy you.' I accordingly fled from Martigny."

"And on the very day, that I went in the opposite direction, as I afterwards learned, madam!"

A burst of sombre laughter accompanied these words of the baronet.

"It is well, sir," was his companion's reply; "then the sin I committed, if it be a sin, had that palliation at least. I left you, very miserable, but carrying with me some consolation,—the child who had come to prove a solace to me in my wretchedness. I went to a distant relative's; the boy grew and loved me; he was placed in the marine, became a man, won his way to the command of a ship by his courage and high character; then I came hither, fearing that you would be led to commit a great sin,—the sin of marrying a second time during the life of your lawful wife."

The baronet grinned.

"Why not, your ladyship? Intent makes sin; and I have not sinned in intent! Did I not believe that you and the boy were lost at sea? That was your device, was it not? *You* conveyed that intelligence to me?"

"I did, sir. It was a sin; but committed to avoid a greater one,—that of remaining with you; and had you believed me and the boy alive, I feared you would pursue us, and force us back."

"And destroy your soul's salvation, my pious spouse."

"Yes; mine and the boy's. I did evil that

good might come of it. You were a heretic and a vicious man; you blasphemed our holy church; had you forced me to return, I should have been compelled to listen to that daily, and worse still, you would have corrupted and poisoned the heart of **the** child. So I originated and had conveyed to you that report of our death. Years passed. I had lied to prevent a terrible impiety; but then came the thought, that my pious fraud would lead you to this sin. You thought me dead; you might marry again; it was my duty to prevent that. So I came hither and watched you, sir; not from love,— I never loved you,— but from a sense of duty. You did not suspect my presence here, but I was near Westbrooke Hall and must have heard of your intended marriage. I have lived poorly; have waited : but for accident you would not have discovered me."

The voice was silent.

"Well, you have related an entertaining history, madam. A misalliance, desertion the solitary life of a recluse on a storm-beaten crag, where your only amusement, I am informed, is to build beacon fires, in the intervals of watching over the morals of your dear spouse,—what could be more romantic, more touching, and ilke the story-books! And may I ask your future intentions, madam?"

"To remain where I am and live as I have lived, sir."

"Ah!"

And the baronet's face grew dark.

"Suppose, in spite of all, I should contract marriage with some second fair one?"

"You dare not!"

"Ah! I warn you I am a tolerably daring person, madam!"

"You will not marry, because you would thereby commit the legal offence of bigamy. The law of God might not restrain you — the law of man would punish you."

"You round your sentences charmingly, madam; but I beg to remind your ladyship of one fact, — that you are supposed to be dead, and even are such on your own authority. Why, then, should I not marry? Widowers, however sad, marry."

"You will not marry, for a good reason, sir."

"What is that, madam, will you please inform me?"

"Because the marriage of Marianne Earle and Sir Murdaugh Westbrooke, baronet, is recorded in the parish register at Martigny, in Normandy!"

The baronet started, and turned pale.

"Fool that I was to forget that!" he muttered; "it is incredible how men will blunder!"

Then looking at his companion sidewise, and with a wary glance,—

"What you say is very true, madam, and I have not the remotest intention of becoming a bigamist," he said.

A keen glance accompanied the last words. The recluse seemed neither to believe or disbelieve them.

"And now to end our interesting conversation, madam. You propose to remain here until I marry?"

"Or I die."

"That would be sad; and as a Catholic you would doubtless confess yourself to a priest?"

"Yes."

"Revealing your true name?"

"My name and whole life."

"So that if I should unfortunately be married, my marriage would be shown to be illegal?"

"Yes."

"It is well," he said, with the spirit of mur-

der in his low voice; "and now for a last point.
Where is that boy?"

The recluse looked intently at him.

"Be at rest — you mean him mischief, unnatural father! but he is beyond your reach."

"Where?"

"I will not reply!"

"Beware how you defy me!" he said, advancing a step toward her.

"I fear you not!"

"Answer!"

"I will not!"

He seized her wrists furiously.

'Reply! or —!"

"Kill me, if you please!" said the woman,
coldly, and exhibiting no signs of pain. "Do
you think I value my life? I despise your
threats and violence, and will tell you nothing,
though you murder me!"

She wrenched her hands from him.

"Go!" she said, rising to her full height;
"the boy has never wronged you. It is I, if
any one, who should suffer."

"And I swear you shall!" howled the baronet; "at present I have *that* to attend to. I
will not give up the search yet. I go now,
but beware of me when I return!"

With these words he hastened from the hut, and rapidly descended the path taken by Wilde and the men.

In ten minutes, such was his haste, he reached the clump of trees in which they waited beside their horses.

"Mount!" he ordered.

The men threw themselves into the saddle.

The baronet and Wilde rode in front, at full gallop.

"He is at Maverick House!" said the former, hoarsely; "and to-night may end that matter, Wilde. But I have other work for you! Be ready to set out for France at daylight."

"Yes, sir."

"You were at Martigny with me — you remember?"

"Yes, sir."

"Well, listen now to my instructions, and see that you obey them to the letter. If you succeed — a thousand pounds sterling! If you fail, find some other master. Now listen!"

And in rapid words he gave the man his instructions as they went on at full gallop.

As the baronet ended, Maverick House glimmered before them in the moonlight a quarter of a mile distant.

"The time is near!" he said; "no faltering, Wilde! this man must die!"

And turning to the men, —

"The desperado we are in search of is here!" he said, "and ready to resist. At the signal from me, fire on him! Shoot him down — a hundred guineas to the man who kills him!"

CHAPTER III.

WHAT ONE WOMAN IS CAPABLE OF TOWARD ANOTHER.

AN hour or two before, Ellinor and Rose Maverick had issued forth, and strolled over the russet lawn, to enjoy the mild and caressing airs of the autumn evening. It was what is called "St. Martin's Summer." The breeze was soft, and fanned their foreheads like the zephyrs of spring. The cutting blasts had not whirled the brown leaves from the trees. The year was going to his death in his trappings of golden sunsets; mists curled around the headlands; the moonlight, mixing with the orange tint in the west, slept serenely on the charming landscape.

The two girls had wandered some distance in the shrubbery.

The superb beauty of Ellinor was unchanged.
Her dark eyes sparkled with satirical wit, her
lips curled with irony, and the magnetic glances
kept for the male sex had given way to an expression best described as "spiteful."

Rose was much altered. The delicate carna-
tion of her cheeks had disappeared. She walked over the russet turf with slow and languid
steps. It was the pale flower of autumn beside
the dazzling rose of summer, and the summer
flower seemed to be amusing herself at the expense of the autumn primrose.

"What a very romantic affair! Who would
ever have believed it ?" said Ellinor, satirically.
"The elegant and high-born Miss Rose Maverick in a love-sick condition about an unknown
adventurer ! "

Rose turned her head impatiently, and a
slight color came to her pale cheeks.

"I have already told you, Ellinor, that it was
unpleasant to me to be spoken to in that manner," she said.

"I don't believe it!" was the reply. It is *not*
unpleasant, my quiet little cousin! You are
proud of your *romance*. Come, confess! *are*
you ashamed of your — well, of your *friendship* for the handsome Mr. Delamere ? "

"I am not," said Rose, firmly. "He saved my life, as he did yours. We owe him friendship, at least—"

"And love? Ah! you wince, my pretty cousin. Your blushes betray you."

Rose Maverick drew herself up with some hauteur, but made no reply.

"Oh! there is your fine air again, my Lady Disdain!" snarled the fair Ellinor. "If you are *not* in love with him, why have you drooped like a flower when the frost comes, ever since that night when he disappeared so mysteriously? Before, your spirits were excellent, and I think the *goody* old people, if not the men, liked you much better than they liked me, preferring your "sweet smile, full of native goodness," one of them said, I remember, "to my brilliant glances." Well, where is the sweet smile? Why do you sit for hours in sad musings? Why have you lost all interest in your flowers, and even forgot to feed your linnet yesterday? I reply that you are in love—in love with the interesting unknown!"

Rose had turned with an offended air to re-enter the house.

Ellinor followed, goading and snapping at her.

"Deny it, if you dare, my romantic cousin!" she said.

Rose made no reply. She walked quietly toward the house, her companion beside her, and laughing maliciously.

"Now you really ought to have taken pattern by my insignificant self," went on her tormentor. "The late interesting Mr. Delamere had the bad taste to prefer me to you. I am penniless, only a poor girl, but he honored me by his attentions; in spite of which I remained quite heart-whole and not in the least *romantic* about the handsome stranger. Oh, he said a number of things to me! Did I never tell you that before? He looked at me in such a way! He told me at last — but here I am becoming indiscreet. If he did not kiss my shoes, and lay his neck down for me to place my foot upon, it was only because he saw that I was too *proper* a young lady to encourage a strange adventurer! There is the blush again, and this time it is an angry blush. Very well, but this is true. He would have knelt down quickly enough, if he had hoped I would raise him up in my arms! And what he *did* do was something! He — "

"I am weary of all this," said Rose, stung to

the quick. " I wonder you take such pains to prove that you are heartless, Ellinor. You are witty and brilliant, you think. Other persons would call your wit ill-temper."

The words went home and aroused in the ironical Ellinor a good old-fashioned fit of pure anger.

" Ah, there you are, my fine cousin!" she cried. " You treat me, as usual, to moral and scriptural abuse. Thank your ladyship! But 'tis enough for the present. I'll go home now and hear the rest of the sermon on another occasion. Thank you!— I am ' ill-tempered'! Oh, yes! And all because I refer to what everybody is speaking of! I say what everybody is speaking of, madam!—your lovesick state of mind all about this unknown stranger, Mr. Delamere! The very neighbors laugh at it! You have no pride, they say. They wonder, as your family wonder, that you should thus honor a person of unknown position and blood, that ever since he disappeared in that mysterious, and, I must say, very suspicious manner, you should have mourned him and cried about him, and loved the very chair he sat in! That is all I have to say, madam! 'Ill-tempered'!"

And the fair Ellinor tossed her head in superb wrath.

"I'd like to know what I have said to expose myself to that insult!" she added. "'Ill-tempered'! and all because I laugh at your infatuation about an adventurer!"

"Mr. Delamere was not an adventurer!" was Rose's cold response.

"What, then, was he? this charming stranger, whose amateur fishing excursions terminated so mysteriously, and so *very* suspiciously."

"I see no mystery and no ground for suspicion in his disappearance," was Rose Maverick's response. "You know as well as I do, Ellinor, that he has been missing since the night of the attack on Westbrooke Hall, when the Viscount Cecil was carried off. It is nearly certain now, as you know equally well, that this attack was made by a party of Frenchmen from a vessel, in the channel, and that their object was to abduct persons of rank to hold as hostages."

"Pray what has that to do with it, if I may address a question without offence to your ladyship?"

"Simply this. Mr. Delamere was returning from his visit here to Oldport, on the night of the attack. On the next morning he had disappeared, and his horse was found grazing in the fields. Nothing further is known; but it is certainly reasonable to suppose that he too was carried off, — since his dress, demeanor, and all connected with him, you will not deny, indicated that he was a gentleman. As such he was worth attention. He was seen no more. Is it so improbable that the French people captured him?"

"A fine theory, indeed!"

"It is at least more charitable than to conclude that he was an adventurer and disappeared as he came, — "mysteriously.""

"You defend your protégé well, madam."

"I take the part of the absent, who are defamed."

"And the absent thanks you!" said a voice in the shrubbery, very near them.

The young ladies recoiled, and uttering exclamations, gazed with affright toward the shadow.

A figure wrapped in a cloak advanced. The face was pale, thin, and worn, but resolute and stern.

It was Earle.

CHAPTER IV.

THE SAILOR AND HIS SHIP.

A SUDDEN and unexpected event was the occasion of Earle's presence at Maverick House.

He had remained prostrate on a couch of illness for weeks after the night of the attack on Westbrooke Hall — the recluse watching over him in the solitary hut with deep solicitude and tenderness.

At last the wound in his shoulder had healed. He had left his sick bed. The fresh breeze of the ocean infused new life into his frame; and seated for hours on the bench in front of the rude cabin on the great headland, he had looked through his glass out on the channel and along the coast.

Where was the corvette? he asked himself.

What had become of his beloved craft? The sailor loves his ship, and the fate of the corvette was ever on Earle's mind. Had she arrived safely with her prize, the viscount, or had she been chased and captured by some English frigate? Was she riding in pride, or sunk fathoms deep beneath the waves of St. George's Channel?

He had been seated in his customary seat on that morning, gazing through his glass and asking himself these questions, when all at once the recluse saw him rise to his feet, and heard him utter an exclamation, almost a cry, of joy.

The corvette was visible in the offing! There was no mistaking the object of his pride and affection! The eye of the sailor knows his craft, as the eye of the lover knows his mistress. There was the corvette slowly beating up toward the coast of Pembrokeshire; and as his mother hastened to his side, Earle pointed the vessel out and exclaimed, —

"There she is, mother!"

"Your ship, my son?" said the poor recluse, not sharing his joy.

"Yes, yes, mother! My own corvette!— coming to rescue her commander."

"Then you will leave me?"

He turned toward her, and looked at her with great tenderness.

"See how strong the sailor spirit is in me: I had not thought of that," he said.

"While I think first of it. You go, and I shall be alone again."

Her voice was full of melancholy, and the sailor's joy was dimmed.

"Come with me, my mother. Leave this wild and lonely spot. Your native Normandy is brighter than this land; come! Nothing there shall ever part us."

"You say *Normandy:* how do you know that Normandy is my birthplace?" said the recluse, suddenly.

"From your missal, mother, — the little book you pray from. I found it on the table near my sick couch, and opened it. On the first leaf is written, ' Marianne Earle, Martigny, Normandy.' "

The recluse was silent.

"Until now I had thought you a native of the South, mother, where we always lived; but you never told me any thing. There will be time, to discuss all this, however. Now time is wanting. See! look through my glass. There is a man; it is Dargonne, on the deck of the corvette.   He has his glass, and is looking for me. He waves his handkerchief, and I reply."

Earle waved his own handkerchief.

"You see, mother!   Get ready to come with me."

"I cannot."

"Why not?"

"I must remain here.   Do not ask me why, my son."

"And we shall part!"

"It breaks my heart, but I must remain, Edmond.   Ask me not why."

"Enough, my mother; I will say no more. Women like yourself never yield.   I must go; but I will return.   My duty calls me now, but we shall still love each other.   See! the signal flags are run up.   I read them as I read print."

"What do they say?"

Earle looked through his glass, and repeated slowly as the fluttering signal flags syllabled the message,—

" Be at — the old place — to-night."

" The recluse sank upon the bench.

" Then it is ended — all my happiness at seeing you near me, my child," she murmured.

And looking at him, she said to herself in a low voice,—

" He does not hear me; he is looking at his vessel, waving his handkerchief. That means that he will be punctual. Oh! why do we love in this world? Why do we become wrapped up in human beings until we are unhappy without them? Then they go — we are alone — our very love works our woe. Alas! my child is going to leave me, and I will be alone."

Earle turned toward her, joyously.

" See! she understands my signal, mother. She has tacked about, content — is making for the coast of Ireland — but she will be here without fail, again, to-night!"

CHAPTER V.

EARLE'S DESIGN.

AS evening approached, Earle dressed himself in his full uniform of a captain in the French navy, buckled on his belt and pistols, and, wrapping his cloak around him, turned to the recluse.

"I am going to be absent for an hour, my mother," he said. "A last duty makes this necessary. Be not afraid: I will soon return, and then I will renew my persuasions to induce you to embark with me for France. Reflect that it will make me very happy, mother; and the good God watch over you."

He left the hut. The recluse had made no response. Bending down and weeping silently, she presented an appearance of the deepest dejection.

Earle threw a last tender glance toward her, and disappeared in the dusk of evening.

He followed the path leading down the headland, in the direction of Maverick House; and just as Sir Murdaugh Westbrooke, with his party, left Westbrooke Hall in pursuit of him, entered the Maverick woods, half a league from the mansion.

As he went on with firm tread, and an expression of stern resolution upon his features, he muttered to himself,—

"Yes: this is a duty, and I will not leave the country without performing it. Chance has placed me in possession of a secret intimately concerning Arthur Maverick, the man who has called me friend, and his household; a murderer is about to enter that household as the husband of one of the family whose head he has assassinated. I alone, besides the gypsy, who has disappeared, can warn the victim. I swear I will do so, and from a sense of duty, not in the least from a mean jealousy; and then, if the marriage takes place, let it take place."

He went on rapidly. Pale and thin as he was, it was evident that his physical vigor was nearly unabated.

"Jealousy!" he muttered as he proceeded

beneath the huge boughs, toward Maverick House, — "jealousy! oh, no! I swear that I am not in the least jealous. The love I had for that woman is dead. She made me crazy for a time; but I have become sane. I can see now — thanks to the hours of meditation and recollec- on my sick couch — that she is false, acted a part with me, lured me on to gratify a poor sentiment of vanity; and when she had en- trapped me, and driven me to an avowal, threw me away without a thought or care for me.

"Fool that I was to imagine that the poor stranger could compete with the rich baronet in madam's eyes. Fool, above all, to give my love to a thing of deception, false as the sea. As the sea? I do it wrong. It is changeable and dangerous, but makes no protestations. You embark on it with a knowledge of its perils. This woman's glance and smile said, 'There is no danger with me.' They fooled me. I was her slave. I am free now; and I am not jealous. Were she to hold out her hand now, I would not take it, for I know her. Fool! to pass by that pure flower, Arthur Maverick's sister, and bestow my love upon this quicksand, Arthur Maverick's cousin. But it is over — all that madness. I care not if she marry the assassin and monster. It is to save Arthur Maverick, my friend, that I go to warn him, and to speak in my own name and character. There is the house, here is the wall : in ten minutes I shall be there."

As he spoke, rapid steps were heard on the path behind him, and he turned round.

Through the dim light a man was seen running towards him, and he drew his pistol.

"Don't shoot, brother. I am a friend !" said the pursuer.

And the gypsy reached him.

"Take care, brother !" he said ; "Sir Murdaugh Westbrooke is on your track !"

CHAPTER VI.

THE WITNESS.

ARLE gazed at the gypsy without exhibiting the least emotion at these words.

"How do you know that?" he said. "But first tell me where you have been?'

"I have been yonder in the woods, in the great ravine beyond Maverick House. On the night of the attack on Westbrooke Hall, I went with you as far as the ledge on the sea shore. There my heart failed me. I heard the shouts of the revenue guard. I was a coward, and glided into the darkness."

"You did well. I have been wounded; but that is no matter. You say I am pursued?"

"Yes, brother. I was at the revenue station to-day, offering to tell fortunes. As I was telling that of the young officer in command, the man Wilde rode up hastily. He brought a note. The officer read it half aloud, and I heard it. It was from Sir Murdaugh Westbrooke, and asked for a party of men to arrest you. You were lurking at a place on the coast near the village of Oldport."

"Ah! he has found out that? And the men were sent?"

"Yes, brother. They were ordered out immediately. Then I left in a hurry, and began to run toward Oldport. As I went, I thought of the hut on the headland, where the solitary woman lives. You might be there, and I went up the steep cliff by a path I found. You were gone; the woman said, had followed the path toward Maverick House. I ran after you, and here I am. The baronet is probably on your track too."

Earle nodded coolly.

" It is well," he said.

He looked keenly at the gypsy, as though to read him through. The look seemed to be understood by the vagabond. His face flushed, and he said,—

" You don't doubt me, brother?"

"No," said Earle, extending his hand; "but this deep interest you show in a stranger—"

"You are no stranger, brother. You are one of the Rommanye Rye. But there is more to make me your friend. You have been kind to me. You have not despised me. All the world despises the gypsies. They are vagabonds and thieves! At their appearance, the housewife takes in her linen from the hedge. When they camp in the woods near a homestead, the farmer looks to his sheep and pigs. They are outcasts; all curse them! I am one of them, and you have been kind, not cruel. You are a gentleman, and have touched my hand and called the poor gypsy ' brother.' That has moved him; he is your friend. I swear to watch over and obey you, brother!"

Earle saw that the speaker was in earnest, and suddenly the thought came, "Here is the witness to the murder."

"You will do what I ask of you, then, brother? " he said.

"I swear it; order me. I am yours!"

"Then follow me. I am going to reveal the murderer of Giles Maverick to his son Arthur. Remain concealed in the shadow of the trees near the house. When I call you, come quickly. See, we are near now. Here is the wall!"

They leaped into the park, and rapidly approached the house.

"Remain here!" said Earle, pointing to a spot in the shrubbery; "and when you hear me blow on my sailor's whistle, come quickly, and give your testimony."

The gypsy made a sign of obedience.

"I will lose no time, brother; and I advise you to hasten. The baronet will not find you on the coast, and will come straight here. I warn you."

"Let him come!"

And Earle rapidly made his way toward the mansion.

Suddenly he heard the sound of voices, and Rose and Ellinor passed in the moonlight. He clearly distinguished what was said; heard the taunts of Ellinor, the charge of loving him, which she brought against her cousin; and heard, too, the defence made of him by Rose.

A moment afterward he stood before them.

11

CHAPTER VII.

THE DENUNCIATION.

CARLE wrapped his cloak around him so as to conceal his uniform, and bowing low to Rose, said, in his deep voice, —

"Once more I thank you, madam. You defend me. The attack is strange!"

He turned to Ellinor.

"I loved you once, or thought I did," he said, coolly. "I love you no longer — have ceased for more than a month to care aught for you. I shall see you no more — before I go I undeceive you on that point, if you have deceived yourself."

Ellinor Maverick blushed crimson at the stern and almost contemptuous words of the sailor. Her pride was cruelly mortified, and anger followed — her eyes darted lightnings.

Before she could speak, however, Earle had turned his back upon her. He went to meet Arthur Maverick, who, startled by the exclamations of the ladies at Earle's appearance, had hurried out to ascertain the cause of their agitation.

"In good time!" said Earle; "it is you whom I come to see."

"Mr. Delamere? Is it possible that you are alive, and not a prisoner either? We thought you had been captured."

"I will explain all, some day," was Earle's reply; "now there is no time. I came not to explain this disapearance, but a much more mysterious affair. My explanation must be brief, the meaning of which statement you willl soon discover, friend."

"Your words astound me!"

"I am about to astound you far more. The object of my hurried visit to-night is to reveal to you what I should have revealed long since."

"To reveal—what?"

"The murderer of your father!"

Arthur Maverick started, and almost recoiled.

"You know the mystery of that terrible affair?"

"Yes!"

"Good heavens, Mr. Delamere! Speak! What frightful intelligence have you to communicate?"

"Intelligence truly frightful! for it reveals a depravity almost incredible. Tell me, friend,— you are that to me,—what think you of love and murder mingled? What would you say if I told you that your father's murderer aspires to an alliance with one of your own family! What if the man whose hands reek with the blood of the uncle, comes to ask the hand of the niece, hopes to make Miss Ellinor Maverick his wife?"

Arthur gazed at the speaker with distended eyes.

Ellinor Maverick, as pale as death, now, seemed about to faint.

"You would say—you surely do not mean—?" Arthur said in a low and agitated voice.

"I mean that Sir Murdaugh Westbrooke, of Westbrooke Hall, is the murderer of Giles Maverick, your father!"

For a moment a deep silence reigned throughout the entire group. The words seemed to paralyze the listeners, and to deprive them of the power of utterance.

The first person who spoke was Ellinor Maverick. She sprang forward with the fury of a tigress.

"Who are *you*, sir?" she cried, white with rage, "who bring this accusation? who are you — the unknown adventurer who dare to assault the character of a gentleman of rank? Speak! *I* will defend Sir Murdaugh, if my cousin is too cowardly to do so!"

Earle bowed with ironical ceremony.

"I compliment you, madam, upon your chivalric defence of the absent. It seems, then, that you can defend as well as attack those who are not present to take their own parts!"

"Answer! no evasion! No trick to avoid a reply to my question!" exclaimed the young lady, stung to wild fury.

"Your question, madam?"

"Who are *you*, I demand, who sneak here to destroy a *gentleman's* character?"

Earle threw back his cloak, and revealed his full uniform of a French captain.

"I am Edmond Earle, of the French navy; an enemy, but an officer and a gentleman! I came to avow that; you hasten the avowal. Yes," he said, turning to the astonished Arthur, "I am not Mr. Delamere, but Captain Earle. I have assumed a part—it was repugnant, but it was done in compliance with orders. French civilians were seized on the French coast— I came to seize English civilians on the English coast! It was I who attacked Westbrooke Hall and, carried off the Viscount Cecil,—it was I who was pursued and wounded on the sea-shore. I have remained here since that time; my ship has returned for me, and the boat is now waiting; but I have come here, risking my life, you see, with a mounted party on my track, to say, ' Thanks for your hospitality friends! I never betrayed that. Before I go, I perform a duty; act as your best friend would act — reveal the fact that a murderer, the murderer of your own father, is about to enter your family as the husband of a member of that family.' "

Arthur Maverick looked and listened with stupefaction. Words seemed to fail him.

" The avowal of my real character is dangerous, perhaps," said Earle; " but I swore I would make it. I am a French officer, and politically your enemy; but personally, my heart beats with earnest affection for you. Do not remember that I am an enemy — think me your friend. There is little time left. Let me hasten and prove my charges."

He made the signal agreed upon, and the gypsy appeared quickly.

"This man is a vagabond, and you may not credit him," said Earle; "but listen to his story first, and form your opinion."

At a sign from Earle the gypsy rapidly narrated the scene at the pool in the forest, more than five years before. As he painted in vivid colors the sombre event which he had witnessed,—the meeting of the enemies, the apparently friendly greeting, the sudden stab, the dog leaping at the murderer's throat, and the murdered man beaten with fragments of rock, and his body dragged to and sunken in the pool,—as this terrible scene was depicted in the forcible words of the gypsy, Arthur Maverick shuddered, and his face assumed the ashy hue of a corpse.

"You do not believe that, perhaps," said Earle, as the gypsy terminated his narrative. "You may say that I am the rejected suitor of Miss Maverick, and have suborned this man to perjure himself, in order to ruin my rival. So be it! form that theory, and try this narrative by the

strongest test. Believe nothing until it is ac-
counted for upon reasonable grounds; and first,
was there no reason why Sir Murdaugh Westbrooke should hate your father?"

"I know of none," said Arthur Maverick in
a stifled voice.

"*I* am better informed!"

"You?"

"Your father bound and lashed the baronet
as men lash a dog! Were you too young to
know that fact? Interrogate your memory."

"Good heavens! And it was my father, then,
who committed that terrible outrage, with which
the whole country rang! Is it possible? and
yet, it is incredible, but —"

"Had they not quarreled?"

"Yes, yes! I now recall old stories of a violent scene between them. They were on a race-
course; had an altercation; my father gave Sir
Murdaugh the lie, and the baronet struck him
with his riding-whip. Before he could repeat
the blow, the bystanders interposed and forced
Sir Murdaugh from the ground!"

"That is enough," said Earle, coolly; "and the
chain of *motive* is perfect. Your father quar-
rels with the baronet, the baronet inflicts a terri-

ble indignity upon Mr. Maverick; the result is that your father returns the insult in kind by binding and lashing his adversary; and the fifth act of the drama is the murder of your father by that adversary."

CHAPTER VII.

THE BLOOD-HOUND.

ARTHUR Maverick's eyes were fixed upon the ground. His expression of horror and astonishment began to give place to a gloomy rage.

"Then, if this be true, I have welcomed and touched the hand of my father's murderer!" he muttered.

Before Earle could reply, Ellinor Maverick bounded toward them.

White with fury, chiefly from the undisguised contempt of her former lover, she caught Arthur by the arm, almost shook him in her rage, and half hissed through her closed set teeth, —

"Do you believe that spy and liar?"

(170)

Arthur Maverick drew back and extricated his arm from her grasp.

"Permit me to manage my own affairs madam, and believe or disbelieve as seems good to me," he said, coldly.

"Believe as you will, then!" was the furious response; "disgrace your name if you will, by giving credit to this convicted spy and adventurer! But you shall not poison *my* mind against —"

"Your uncle's murderer, madam? As you will — that is your affair. I arrogate no authority over you. But listen to me. I am the head of the house of Maverick in Pembrokshire; my father was murdered; a man is charged with the murder. I will pursue the inquiry to the last limits. If true, the guilty shall suffer. If untrue, the innocent will be vindicated. Does that suit your views, madam? If not, the fact will not move me."

Ellinor was carried away by her rage.

" I say the very idea is an insult!"

" So be it, madam. People will be insulted, then."

" It is an outrage — a thing unheard of, that this unknown adventurer, this man who dared to pay his addresses to me, whom I spurned and laughed at, and ordered to leave my presence, — it is infamous that on *his* testimony a gentleman of rank and character should be suspected!"

"She fights hard for her rich suitor!" muttered Earle, with stern irony.

And then raising his voice, —

"May I call your attention to one fact, madam?" he said, coldly: "I have no testimony to give."

"You have paid this vulgar wretch to blacken Sir Murdaugh!"

"I am too poor, madam!"

He made her a mock inclination, and spoke with an accent of such contempt that the lady shuddered with rage, and with difficulty refrained from springing at him.

"To end this scene," said Earle, returning to his gloomy tone, full of sternness and cold resolution: "I expected this reception — I was thus prepared for it, and it does not move me. I had my duty to perform, and have performed it, — at some risk, too," he said to Arthur Maverick. "Do you doubt that? Listen!"

He raised his finger, and there was dead silence for a moment.

In the midst of this silence rapid hoof-strokes were heard on the road leading to the great gate.

" Do you hear ? " said Earle, coolly.

" Yes ! " was Arthur Maverick's reply — " the meaning of that sound ? "

" Sir Murdaugh Westbrooke is coming hither with a party to seize and murder me."

" The baronet ? "

" In person ! Can you not fancy the worthy's motive ? On the night when this black mystery was revealed to me, he had me tracked — his secret emissary overhead all. Sir Maudaugh *knows that I know* — his good name is threatened. I may send him to the gallows — he has doomed me — and is coming to murder me ! "

The hoof-strokes sounded nearer, and a shudder ran through Rose Maverick, who was standing pale but erect beside her brother.

" My sentence is already pronounced ; I am to die," said Earle, coolly; " and I lose my life by coming hither to warn you of this man's character ! Does that prove, or does it not, that *I* believe this gypsy's statement ? He alone can speak of that scene — ".

Earle suddenly stopped.

The hoof-strokes clashed on the avenue. The pursuers were nearly upon them.

"Yes, yes!" said Earle: "there is another witness — and he is here! the blood-hound! — you informed me that he was still alive, old and blind nearly. Send for the dog! — he will know the murderer!"

"I will go for him in person! wait!"

And Arthur Maverick disappeared at a bound toward the rear of the mansion, where the bloodhound — dangerous in spite of his great age — was kept chained.

As his figure disappeared, Sir Murdaugh Westbrooke rushed toward the group. Behind came his men, ready to obey his orders.

"There he is!" shouted the baronet, "armed and ready to resist!"

Earle's pistol was indeed in his hand, and unconsciously he raised it.

"He is ready to fire! Shoot him down!" cried the baronet furiously.

And he raised his own pistol, but suddenly let it fall.

Rose Maverick had rushed between Earle and the threatening muzzle.

"You dare not fire upon *me!*" she exclaimed disdainfully; "if you dare — fire!"

And beautiful, superb, her cheeks burning with passionate feeling, —

" I *know* now that you murdered my father!" she exclaimed.

Tne words were nearly drowned in a hoarse and threatening roar; and an instant afterwards an enormous blood-hound bounded down the steps.

At sight of the dog, Sir Murdaugh Westbrooke uttered a hoarse cry and turned to fly.

It was too late. The dog had recognized the murderer of his master. IIis bloodshot eyes glared at the baronet for an instant; his huge mouth opened wide, displaying the jagged teeth — then with one bound the blood-hound reached the spot and sprung at his enemy's throat.

A second cry, hoarse and horror-stricken like the first, came from the baronet. But this time it was suddenly interrupted. The hound's teeth were on his throat. A supernatural strength seemed to animate the faithful animal — the baronet struggled in vain — suddenly man and dog fell beneath the trampling hoofs of the horses, and Earle's voice was heard exclaiming, —

" Behold the murderer of Giles Maverick!"

As he uttered the words the far boom of cannon came from the channel.

Earle started.

It came a second time. The omnious sound was unmistakable.

"The corvette!—she is attacked!" cried Earle.

And seizing the bridle of the baronet's horse, he leaped into the saddle.

"Farewell, friends!" he cried to Arthur and Rose: "there are my cannon!—I know their ring! My corvette is fighting and I am absent! Farewell!"

And charging, pistol in hand, the confused revenue guard, he passed through them, followed only by a few random shots, and then disappeared toward the coast.

CHAPTER IX.

WHAT FOLLOWED.

CARLE went on at full speed.

The boat, he knew, awaited him at the cove under the headland: to reach the spot now without delay was the one thought that possessed him.

The animal he bestrode was a powerful hunter, of the purest blood and the highest speed. At every bound he cleared ten feet. Earle drove him on mercilessly. With erect head, floating mane, and foam flying from his jaws, he darted straight on toward the coast, along whose headlands and rocky promontories reverberated the hoarse boom of the cannon.

Suddenly another sound mingled with the far ominous roar, — the smiting of hoofs on the road behind.

Earle turned his head and listened.

'They are following me," he muttered, digging the spur into his horse's sides.

He was not mistaken. Sir Murdaugh Westbrooke was on his track.

A brief but fiery scene had followed the fall of the baronet, in the clutch of the blood-hound. His men ran to him, dragged off the dog, and he rose to his feet, trembling, bleeding, and as pale as a corpse.

" The meaning — of — this — outrage ? " he gasped.

" Ask your memory," was Arthur Maverick's response, in a low, hoarse tone.

He advanced close to the baronet as he spoke, and fixed his eyes upon him.

" You are the murderer of my father ! " came in a low hiss through his pale lips.

The baronet recoiled, and his eyes seemed starting from their cavernous sockets.

" That hound convicts you ! See ! I have only to step aside and he will tear you to the earth a second time ! Wretch ! murderer ! convicted assassin ! your black crime shall not go unpunished longer !"

And catching the baronet by the throat, he would have strangled him despite his great strength, had not the men forcibly interposed, and parted them instantly.

"It — is — well!" gasped the baronet, staggering back; "you shall answer for this outrage. I go now, but I return. My horse!"

And turning, he caught almost mechanically, the bridle of a horse which one of the men hastened to lead forward.

The baronet mounted hastily, and made a sign to his men to do likewise.

Arthur Maverick seemed to hesitate whether he would attempt to retain him or not.

"Well, go!" he said; "but beware how you set your foot here again. Return, as you say you will, and you die by my hand."

The baronet looked at the speaker with eyes full of indescribable rage, with which was mingled no little trepidation.

"It is well!" he said, in a low tone; "but let the son beware of the fate of the father."

As he spoke he turned his horse's head, and struck the spur into the animal's sides.

"Come!" he shouted in hoarse tones to the men; "we may catch up with the spy yet. A hundred guineas for his head!"

And he set out at full speed on the track of

Earle.   The men followed, and the party disappeared like a whilwind.

The dismounted man, whose horse the baronet rode, ran after them.

The gypsy had already disappeared.

CHAPTER X.

THE FLAG WITH THE LILIES.

EARLE continued his flight, making straight for the coast.

The hunter cleared the earth with long strides, and promised very soon to distance all pursuit and reach the strand.

Suddenly he staggered. A sharp stone had entered his foot, and inflicted a deep wound. Such was the pain that he was unable to keep up his great speed; his pace fell off; he limped terribly; and Earle heard behind him the shouts of the pursuers, who every moment were gaining upon him.

He turned and looked over his shoulder; then through the night mist toward the coast. From the rear came threatening cries; from the front, the long reverberating boom of cannon from the channel.

Behind that curtain of white mist wrapping the shores and the great headlands, Earle felt that a hard combat was going on between his corvette and an English frigate probably.

The thought drove him to frenzy almost. He struck the poor animal he rode, with his clenched fist.

"Faster! faster!" he exclaimed. "I care not for myself. But she is attacked yonder — my corvette! They are fighting, and I am not there!"

With merciless spur, he drove the animal to full speed, in spite of his wound; and thus pursuers and pursued swept onward toward the sea.

It was now a race for life. The party commanded by Sir Murdaugh Westbrooke were every moment gaining on the sailor. Either they caught glimpses of him, or heard the sound of his horse's hoofs. They came closer and closer, and Earle heard them, and prepared for the worst.

As his horse went on at full speed nearly, in spite of the painful limp, the sailor slipped his belt round, and placed the handle of his pistol where he could easily grasp it.

"If they come up, I will fight them all," he muttered, with his short, defiant laugh. "That is not brave; it is the only course! If I am arrested, I will die on the gallows. Yes, my good Sir Murdaugh Westbrooke, you play with edged tools. You may come up with me, but *you* come to your death!"

A pistol-shot was heard, and a bullet whistled by his head. He drew his own weapon, but did not fire.

"I am too good a sailor to waste my shot," he muttered.

And he went on, pursued by cries; they evidently saw him, and were gaining rapidly on him.

The mist opening for a moment, gave him all at once a full glimpse of the party. At their head rode Sir Murdaugh, and Earle heard him howl, —

"Shoot him down! Death to him!"

Then the mist enveloped them.

But from this mist came, nearer and nearer, the hoof-strokes and the cries. Earle's horse staggered under him, and seemed about to fall.

From the front, as before, came the thunder of cannon, and with this now mingled the hoarse dash of the waves.

"The coast is near. I cannot see, but there is the sound a sailor knows," muttered Earle.

The roll of the surf grew louder. With it came now the confused sound of voices.

Earle's brows were heavily knit.

"I had forgotten that!" he exclaimed. "While I am followed by this party, bent on my death, another party awaits me yonder. Between the two I shall be crushed!"

The wind whirled away the mist, and on the strand were seen confused shapes, — men running to and fro.

"I have mistaken my route, and am near Oldport," muttered Earle.

Then gazing before him, —

"If these people see me, I am lost!" he exclaimed.

As he spoke, the party behind rushed upon him, with fierce shouts. From the mist emerged a whirlwind of furious enemies, pistol in hand.

"Halt! or you are dead!"

Earle replied by firing at the baronet.

The bullet passed through his hat. Only a moment afterwards a hail-storm of balls whistled around the sailor.

His horse had struck his wounded foot, and, half falling, saved the life of his rider.

The bullets passed over Earle's head, and the baronet uttered a cry of rage.

"Ride him down! See, his horse will carry him no farther!"

Earle drove the spur deep into his animal's side. The only result was that the horse uttered a groan, and nearly fell.

At the same moment violent hands caught the bridle, and threw him on his haunches.

"Who be you?" cried a voice — the voice of the man in front.

Earle recognized that voice. It belonged to Goliath.

He threw himself from the saddle.

"I am one of the wolves!" he said; "and they are after me!"

"You!" exclaimed the giant, recognizing him.

"Yes: listen! Yonder are the men who are hunting me down!"

The baronet rushed on with his men, who uttered shouts of triumph.

"Who be these?" said Goliath.

"Sir Murdaugh Westbrooke and the revenue guard!"

No sooner had Goliath heard Earle's reply, than he drew a long knife. His next proceeding was to utter a shrill and prolonged cry, resembling the scream of the sea-gull.

At that cry, dusky shapes rushed toward him from every direction. The wolves had evidently recognized the signal, which meant, " One of the wolves is in danger ! "

" You be safe, master," said Goliath.

Earle drew his second pistol.

" Go on, master ; where you be going? "

" I am not going anywhere ! "

As he spoke, the pursuers darted upon them.

" Kill him ! " exclaimed the baronet, " and all who resist ! "

As he spoke he fired at Earle, and, riding at him, levelled a blow at him with his pistol, which was still smoking.

The sailor parried it, and fired on the baronet, so close that the powder blackened his face. As the weapon was discharged, the horse ridden by the baronet took fright and wheeled. He was not destined to bear off his rider, however, who had remained uninjured. One of the wolves caught the baronet by the throat and dragged him down. Then the fight surged over him. Quick pistol-shots, cries, the revenue guards scattering and flying, hotly pursued, — such were the sounds and sights which greeted Sir

Murdaugh as he rolled to the earth, and a powerful wolf placed his knee on him.

" Quick, master," said Goliath to Earle ; " the fight be over ! take care of yourself ! "

" Thanks."

And Earle caught a horse and threw himself into the saddle.

" Good-by, brother ! " he said, grasping the huge · hand of Goliath ; " you have saved my life to-night, and I shall not forget that."

Goliath shook his head.

" No need of thanking me, master. You be a wolf, but look out ! "

Earle turned in the direction indicated by the giant's finger.

The sound of cavalry coming on at full gallop was heard.

" The revenue station people ! "

" They are too, late ! "

And with a last pressure of the hand, Earle darted off along the shore toward the spot where the boat awaited him.

In ten minutes he stopped, and threw himself to the earth.

Then he began to run along the narrow ledge of rock, and disappeared in the shadow of the headland.

Ten minutes afterwards the revenue guard who had ridden down to the shore, might have been heard uttering cries.

A boat had darted from the shadow of the headland, above which suddenly soared the beacon light. The gigantic torch lit up all. The ruddy glare turned night into day. The boat was rowed by four men, and another in uniform stood erect in the stern.

A shower of bullets from the guard, who rode down into the surf, greeted the boat.

The reply aroused furious shouts and more shots.

It was simple.

The man in the stern unfurled a flag, and waved his hat.

The glare of the beacon fell on the flag.

On its defiant folds were emblazoned the lilies of France; and, as though, to salute it, a salvo of cannon roared from the channel.

Earle waved his hat a second time in triumph, and in ten minutes the boat had disappeared in the mist.

PART III.

BURIED ALIVE.

—•••—

CHAPTER I.

BARON DELAMERE.

NTIL nearly midnight the cannon continued to roar from St. George's Channel; then the dull sound receded, was heard at intervals only; then ceased.

Three days afterwards His French Majesty's corvette the *Solitaire*, entered the port of Brest, having in tow His Britannic Majesty's sloop-of-war the *Hornet*, which had attacked the corvette in St. George's Channel, off the coast of Pembrokeshire, and very nearly succeeded in sinking the Frenchman.

In fact the fight was plainly going in favor of the *Hornet*, and the corvette was trying to get off, when a boat rowed by four sailors, with a fifth person standing in the stern, was seen making its way from shore, directly under the fire of the *Hornet's* guns — and this boat in the midst of plunging shot, and a fire of musketry directed at it, reached the corvette; the person in the stern leaping instantly upon deck, and, as the English commander could see, taking command.

From that moment the fight became far more obstinate; and it was soon obvious that whoever the commanding officer of the corvette might be, he had resolved to go to the bottom rather than strike his flag. Success crowned his hard work — it was the sloop-of-war which struck her flag, and the corvette sailed away with her, managing to evade the English cruisers and reach Brest in safety.

Such had been the result of Earle's night combat in St. George's Channel, — victory over a waspish craft manned by good men, and commanded by a brave old sea-dog. He sailed into Brest with colors flying, and was saluted by the fortress with the roar of cannon.

An hour afterwards he had cast anchor.

His barge was manned, and he sprung into it. The oars fell, the barge danced over the waves, Earle touched shore; and was soon bowing, cocked hat in hand, in presence of the great Duc de Choiseul, prime minister, who chanced, happily for the sailor's fortunes to be on a visit to Brest, and to witness his triumphal entry.

A week afterwards Captain Edmond Earle was travelling post from Paris to the village of Martigny.

The object of his visit was to procure a copy of his baptismal register, and the formal record of the marriage of his father and mother.

These documents were necessary before he could be created Baron Delamere.

That was the reward designed to be conferred on the young sailor; and for the suggestion he was indebted to no less a personage than the Viscount Cecil.

A few words will place the reader in possession of the details. Our history passes in Wales, and only touches for a few moments the French shore.

The capture of the viscount had pleased everybody, and the court was thus in high good humour. He was released at once on parole; fêted by the anti-war party; received with great politeness by his grace the Duc de Choiseul, . whose word was law throughout France; and one morning when he was shown into the minister's cabinet he found Earle in waiting.

"Ah! you have returned then, my dear Captain?" he said.

"As you see, my lord," said Earle, bowing.

"And, I have heard, with a prize. What ship had the bad luck to meet you?"

"I was attacked by His Britannic Majesty's sloop-of-war *Hornet*, my lord."

"Commanded by Digby! You had a hard fight?"

"A very hard one, my lord. Captain Digby did not seem to know when he ought to strike! A very brave man!"

The Viscount Cecil bowed.

"When one brave sailor speaks well of another, we civilians should listen."

"Your lordship does me great honor."

"Not more than you deserve, sir. Come to England — I will have you made a peer!"

The Duc de Choiseul laughed.

"What say you, Monsieur le Capitaine?"

The sailor bowed.

“ I have a flag, my lord. It is the flag of the lilies ! ”

The viscount approached the duke.

“ See, monseigneur! you have a nobleman already made there.”

“ But you think, my Lord Viscount — ” said Choiseul.

“ That you should make him a baron, at least, monseigneur.”

“ Baron — whom ? ”

“ Stay: I find you a name, monseigneur. Delamere — *de-la-mer.* He captured me while bearing that name; and I assure your lordship that he will honor your patent.”

The Duc de Choiseul inclined politely.

“ Will it oblige Monsieur le Vicopte ? ”

“ Very greatly, my lord. It is a great privilege to be able to reward merit — I have enjoyed it at times.”

The duke took a large sheet of paper, wrote some lines upon it, and then affixed his seal to it.

“ Monsieur le Baron Delamere,” he said, turning to Earle, “ take this paper to the Bureau of Record, which you will easily find, and have all the formalities attended to by the

13

chief of the Bureau. You will then report in fifteen days to the admiral at Brest for orders. The *Tèmèraire* will await you there, and you will take command of her!"

Earle bowed low. The *Tèmèraire* was a frigate of the first class; and he was dizzy for joy. He did not think of the paper in his hand. But when he found himself in the antechamber he glanced at it.

"Edmond Earle — created — by His Majesty —for important services — Baron Delamere. Choiseul."

Earle read something like that. The whole affair astonished him. And he owed this latter distinction to his brave enemy the viscount!

As he walked on, in a dream as it were, he felt a hand laid upon his arm.

He turned quickly. It was the Viscount Cecil.

"Farewell, baron; I return to England to-morrow," said the viscount.

"You are released, then, my lord?"

"Yes."

"I am overjoyed to be so informed. It was by my act that you have been thus inconvenienced — and your revenge has been princely, my lord."

The viscount took the sailor's arm, and they walked on together.

"Listen, my dear Captain Earle — for that is your most honorable title," said Viscount Cecil: "I am an old man now, and have seen a great deal of the world. I never prided my on many things, but I think I recognize a gentleman whenever I meet one. Well, you conducted yourself as such in capturing me, and you beat Digby — those two facts have much impressed me. To day I found the occasion — his grace was in an excellent humor. He has made you a baron — you deserve that, sir; and when the war ends, come and see me. I live at Wentworth Castle — you will always be welcome there. Farewell, Captain! There is the Bureau of Record."

And he held out his hand, which Earle pressed warmly.

"Thanks, my lord," he said. "The king ennobles me for a fight and a victory. But there are others who do not require that, since they are noblemen by nature."

And they parted, — Earle entering the Bureau.

He was ushered into an inner apartment, where a dry-looking individual scowled at him.

At sight of the paper in the writing of Choiseul, however, this individual dissolved into profuse politeness.

"Will Monsieur le Baron be seated?" he said, bowing and pointing to a chair. "This patent is in regular order. I congratulate Monsieur le Baron. A few formalities only are necessary, — mere formalities; namely, the full name of Monsieur le Baron's father and mother, and the date of their marriage; also, the date of Monsieur le Baron's birth: that will be all. Delighted to serve Monsieur le Baron!"

And the functionary executed another bow.

Earle responded in the same manner, and left the Bureau, with "Monsieur le Baron" fairly ringing in his ears.

On the next morning he set out for Martigny, in Normandy, remembering the writing in the recluse's missal.

Just at dusk he reached the village.

As he entered it in the post-carriage, a man muffled in a heavy overcoat passed, running rapidly.

The man seemed making for the sea-coast, a mile or so distant, where some sail-boats were seen.

Earle scarcely looked at him. He stopped

at the inn, and was directed to the house of the curé.

"What is your pleasure, my son?" said the old priest, meeting him on the steps.

"To see your register, father, and find the date of the marriage of the *Tèmèraire!* Pshaw!—pardon, father! They have-given me a frigate, and it has turned my head!"

CHAPTER II.

THE MUTILATED REGISTER.

TWO hours before the appearance of Earle at the village of Martigny, a man of powerful frame, his face half-covered by a heavy beard, had knocked at the door of the old priest's house, and, receiving the reply " Come in," had entered.

" You are the priest of this parish ? " said the man, with a foreign accent.

" Yes, my son."

" And you have in your possession the record of births in the parish ? "

" Yes, my son."

" I wish to examine them, — to find the registry of the birth of Jean Angely, cordwainer," said the man.

The old priest mildly inclined his head.

"That will be easy, my son. But you know we poor priests are very curious, having so little to amuse us. The object of this inquiry, my son?"

"That Jean Angely may inherit property left to him. His cousin, Guillaume Angely, of Tours, leaves a farm to Jean Angely, born at Martigny, and son of Robert Angely and Suzanne, his wife. The fact of his birth needs formal proof. The register will prove it."

The priest inclined his head, and, after a moment's hesitation, opened a closet. From this he took a large volume in black leather, and laid it on the table.

"The date is about 17—," said the man.

"An error of a year, my son."

"It may be."

And the man turned over the leaves, examining the register.

As he was thus engaged, a second knock came at the door.

"Come in!" repeated the old priest, and a child entered.

"Well, my little one?"

The child modestly held down his head and said,—

"Mother Francois is dying, and wishes to see you, father."

"Mother Francois! Dying! Why, she was scarcely ill!"

He rose quickly and put on his hat. Then he stopped, looking toward the man.

Compassion conquered, however, and he went toward the door.

"I will return speedily, my son. Await my coming."

And he left the room.

As the door closed, the man turned round and listened attentively. The priest's footsteps receded.

"Good!" he said; "my little trap has caught the old bird. I have ten minutes."

With a sharp knife he rapidly cut from the volume one of the leaves. This he examined a second time, to be sure that no mistake had been made, folded, and placed in his pocket-book; returned the latter to his pocket; and, taking pen, ink, and paper, carefully copied the entry in the register, relating to Jean Angely, cordwainer.

He was thus occupied when the old priest returned, red in the face, and looking much mortified.

"These children! these children!" he murmured: "to think of Emile Drouet playing a trick on me."

The man raised his head.

"They played a trick, do you say?" he inquired.

"Yes, yes, my son; Mother Francois was much better than when I saw her this morning, and had never sent Emile. That child will turn out badly."

"A young rascal!" said the man. "Well, I have copied the entry I wish, and you can attest it."

"I will do so with pleasure, my son."

And comparing the copy of the entry, it was found correct. The old priest then certified on the paper that it was a true copy, signed his name, and the man folded up the document, and put it in his pocket.

"Is any fee to be paid?" he asked.

"None, my son. It is my duty to keep the register, and afford access to it. I can even offer you a part of my poor dinner, if it please you to share it."

This the man declined, and wrapping a great overcoat around him, he straightway left the priest's house.

He did not go to the inn, but out toward the suburbs, in the direction of the coast.

Once in the suburbs, he began to run, making for a clump of woods on a hill.

He saw a post-carriage driving rapidly into Martigny from the direction of Paris.

He scarcely glanced at it, and reaching the woods, disappeared.

CHAPTER IIХ

THE day seemed destined to be a busy one for the good priest of Martigny. .

The man who had called to examine the record of the birth of Jean Angely, had scarce left him, when another appeared, anxious to know "the date of the marriage of the *Tèmèraire*."

Earle laughed, and corrected himself.

"I mean the date of the marriage of one who was probably a member of your flock, father."

"Her name, my son?"

"Marianne Earle."

The old priest looked up quickly.

"Marianne Earle, my son?" he said.

"Yes, father. Did you not know her?"

"As I should know my own child, had I enjoyed the happiness of paternity."

"Then you loved her?"

"Tenderly."

Again the old priest looked intently at Earle.

"Well, father, then you will certainly be pleased to aid me. I am her son."

"You the son of Marianne Earle!"

The sailor nodded.

"Does that seem strange, father?"

"And she sends you?"

Earle shook his head.

"Why, then, do you come?"

Earle explained his object.

The old priest listened, quietly; but it was plain that he was weighing every word which his companion uttered.

"Now you understand, father. Pray look for your register. I wish to find the date of my mother's marriage, and that of my birth too."

The old priest did not move.

"In a moment, my son. Where is your mother now?"

"In Wales."

"You have seen her lately?"

"Yes."

"And she could not inform you of the exact date?"

"Doubtless; but the occasion has just arisen; moreover, she has always preserved a singular silence on these matters."

"Her silence has been judicious, my son," said the old priest, gravely; "I know its cause, and approve it."

"What is the cause?"

"I will tell you frankly. She wishes to preserve you from a knowledge of your father."

"Of my father? Was he not her cousin, Edmond Earle of the Marine?"

The priest hesitated an instant.

"No," he said at length; "he was a heretic."

"My father a heretic!—and not Edmond Earle!—you astound me, father!"

"I tell you the truth, my son; and your mother had good reason to conceal all this. She was one of my flock, and I knew every thought of her heart. Every breath she drew was purity itself, and she placed her religious duties before all. Your father would surely have corrupted you—hence she fled to rescue you. Now you come and ask me to tell you, in effect the name of that father. Do you wonder I hesitate?"

Earle pondered with knit brow for a moment.

"No father — but — it is astounding! Edmond Earle not my father? His name, then! his name! Or rather let me see the register!"

The old priest said solemnly, —

"Swear to me, that you will not be corrupted by him, my son."

"Corrupted?"

"That you will not permit him to shake your faith in the Holy Church."

"I swear it, father. I am a good Catholic, and will die in the true faith! Does that satisfy you? My father's name now?"

"Sir Murdaugh Westbrooke."

CHAPTER IV.

THE DISCOVERY.

CARLE gave a violent start and turned so pale that he seemed about to faint.

"Sir Murdaugh Westbrooke!" he gasped, — "that man my father!"

"Yes!"

"You laugh at me, old man! My father was a French sailor, Edmond Earle, a brave man and a good Catholic."

"You are mistaken. Your father was an Englishman, and I am sorry to say a heretic, my son!"

"Good heavens!"

The old priest assumed an expression which said, —

"It is melancholy, but true!"

Then he added in words, —

"You doubtless have seen him?"

"Yes," said the sailor, in a low voice; his brows knit, his eyes fixed upon the carpet.

"Without knowing of the relationship?"

"I never dreamed of it," said Earle, in the same tone.

Then rising suddenly, and losing sight apparently of the presence of the priest, he paced hurriedly up and down the room, exclaiming at intervals, —

"That man my father! — the husband of my mother, living there within sight of her; never acknowledging, or perhaps not knowing her! It is incredible, or it is infamous! That murderer whom I have just renounced! that man who has tracked, and hunted me to my death well-nigh! that assassin, that infamous excrescence of humanity, — this wretch my father! my own father!"

He sank into a chair, and covered his face with both hands. His breast shook, a deep sob tore its way from his lips, and scalding tears trickled between his fingers.

The old priest went to him, and said soothingly, —

"Do not be so much moved, my son. No human being can control his fate. It is not your fault that you are this man's son. Dry your tears; seek consolation where alone it is to be found, and all will once more grow peaceful in your breast. Lift up your heart!"

The old man man raised his hand, and pointed toward heaven. Earle slowly inclined his head, and removed his hands. His face was wet with tears:

"Enough, father," he said. "I was a child for a moment, but I am a man again."

His face flushed. He rose to his feet.

"Yes, a man! and my mother shall not suffer!"

"Your mother?"

"She shall not be repudiated by that man! I know him too well; he has acted infamously, if he is my father; he is bent on acting more infamously still."

"Tell me all, my son."

"He designs marrying a second time; and even now may be perfecting that crime in spite of all I have done to destroy him!"

"You! a second marriage! Why that would be no marriage, since your mother still lives, you say. And you speak of attempting to destroy him! How is all this, my son?"

Earle grew calm, collected, and on his guard all at once. The old priest's foible was evidently curiosity; but the sailor did not wish to gratify this curiosity. A heavy weight was on his heart, and he saw that there was no time to lose if he meant to act.

"I am in haste now, father," he said, "and must reserve my story for another occasion. At present I request that you will exhibit to me your register, and supply me with an attested copy of the marriage record of Marianne Earle and Sir Murdaugh Westbrooke. It is here — the register?"

"Yes, my son; there upon the table."

And the old priest approached the table, and opened the volume bound in black leather.

"Another person has just visited me, on an errand similar to yours, my son. His object was to procure a copy, attested, of a certain birth entry. What you wish is further back. It ought to be here," he added, stopping as he turned over the leaves.

He examined the pages.

"Strange!" he said. "I do not find it, and yet — "

He looked at the paging of the volume. At a glance it was evident that one of the sheets was missing, since page 39 followed page 36.

"Can it be?"

And the priest examined the volume more closely. A sheet had been cut out. The narrow strip remained indicating the theft.

"It is incredible! How was it possible? Yes, yes! while I was absent! That was a plan laid to remove me. Not a doubt of it!"

"What is the matter, father?" exclaimed Earle.

"It is gone, my son. The entry of your father and mother's marriage has been stolen!"

"Stolen! By whom?"

"By the man who was here an hour ago."

"The man —!"

"An Englishman, as I conjectured from his accent. He had me sent for on a false errand; remained here, and must have cut out this leaf."

Earle gazed in astonishment at the book, and saw the narrow slip.

"What interest could any one have in —"
Suddenly he stopped.

"An Englishman, did you say, father?"

"As I supposed, my son."

"His appearance?"

"A large man of great bulk and strength, though not tall. He had a heavy black beard on his face, and wore an English dreadnought coat."

"It was Wilde!" exclaimed Earle; "and he was sent hither by his master. This proof of the marriage with my mother existed. He is bent on marrying again, and has abstracted it."

He turned quickly, and seized his hat.

"What route did the man take, father?"

"I can tell you that, my son. He went straight toward the coast."

Earle hastened toward the door.

"Farewell, father! I am going to pursue him. I have fifteen days' furlough; this cloak will conceal my uniform. From this moment it is a struggle which of us shall reach England first. I will have that paper, or the life of the man who carries it on his person. If he arrives with it, all is lost! If I come up with him all is saved. Farewell, father! Your blessing. I go on a dangerous journey."

And turning suddenly, the young man knelt on one knee.

"Heaven bless and prosper you, my son!"

A moment afterwards Earle had disappeared.

CHAPTER V.

THE BLOW OF THE WHIP.

AT the moment when Earle left Paris, on his way to Martigny, events of importance to the personages of this history were occurring in Pembrokeshire.

Arthur Maverick was seated in his library, gloomily reflecting, when a servant entered and announced Sir Murdaugh Westbrooke.

A moment afterwards the baronet entered.

His brow was as black as night, and there was something venomous and yet apprehensive in the glance shot sidewise from his deep-set eyes.

Arthur Maverick rose quickly. His whole person seemed suddenly to have stiffened into stone.

"Your pleasure, sir!" he said, in a voice

which was scarcely recognizable. "What does my father's murderer propose to himself in coming to this house?"

The young man's expression was sick and scornful. It was plain that he tolerated the presence of the baronet only by a strong effort.

"I came to speak of that," was the low reply of Sir Murdaugh Westbrooke; "to ascertain if I am to suffer in the estimation of yourself and the Misses Maverick from the testimony of a vagabond and the attack of a mad dog."

Arthur looked at him fixedly.

"How do you know that the vagabond testified against you?" he said.

Sir Murdaugh Westbrooke was caught.

"I thought as much. He is my enemy and has endevored to extort money from me. He made up the whole of this base charge. Your father and myself never met after our quarrel on the race-course."

"Not even when he bound you to a tree and lashed you?"

Sir Murdaugh quivered with rage at the scornful glance of the young man.

"That is a lie, like the charge of murder. He never so outraged me."

"And you think I will believe you — you, the

convicted liar and murderer!" exclaimed the young man. "You suppose, then, that I am a baby — that because I have not arrested you, you will go free. Undeceive yourself. Your fate approaches. At the next assizes I lay an information against you, and the gallows shall avenge my father."

Sir Murdaugh rose in tremendous wrath.

"Then there are none but enemies here," he growled.

"You have one friend at least," exclaimed a voice at the door, and Ellinor bounded into, rather than simply entered the apartment.

"Yes!" she cried, "there is one person who disbelieves this infamous fabrication, this slander based on the testimony of spies and vagabonds and dogs. My cousin there," and she scornfully pointed towards Authur, "may believe as he chooses, and insult the guests in his own house to his heart's desire; but I, at least, will not do that. I cling to — "

"Your rich suitor, madam?"

And with an expression of overpowering scorn, Arthur Maverick made his cousin a low bow.

The contempt of his voice and expression seemed to sting the fair Ellinor into wild rage.

"If I am to be insulted, I will leave this house. I am not homeless; Lady Worsham will protect me."

"As you please, madam," said the young man, making her a second bow of profound ceremony. "You are welcome here as long as you remain Miss Ellinor Maverick. If you design becoming Lady Westbrooke, the ceremony will not take place here."

The young lady could scarce contain her rage at these words.

"Very well, sir," she said, shooting a wrathful glance at her cousin; "will you have the goodness to order a carriage to take me to Lady Worsham's?"

Arthur Maverick quietly rang a bell, and a servant entered.

"The coach!" he said.

The servant disappeared.

"I will not remain here an instant longer than is necessary, sir."

And going out, the young lady banged the door violently after her.

Sir Murdaugh had listened attentively. He had supposed his suit at an end forever. Now the unexpected turn of affairs showed him that he might derive enormous advantage from

Ellinor's continued adhesion to her engagement. Who would be brought to believe that he was a murderer, when Miss Maverick consented to become Lady Westbrooke? Would the niece marry the murderer of her own uncle? No one would believe that. It was with a sudden sentiment of safety and triumph, therefore, that the baronet prepared to depart.

"I will imitate Miss Maverick now, sir, and rid you of my furthur presence here," he said, venomously.

"Do so," said Arthur Maverick, "and beware how you return."

"And you, sir, beware how you insult me," hissed the baronet.

"Insult you? You are not worth insult."

"Beware!"

"This is my reply to you."

And seizing a riding-whip lying on the table near, the young man, in a wild rage at the presence of his father's murderer, struck the baronet a furious blow across the face.

In an instant they would have clutched each other; but the door suddenly flew open.

"The blood-hound, sir!" exclaimed a servant, rushing into the apartment.

"What of the hound?" said Arthur Maverick, pale with passion, and quivering in every muscle.

"There at the door, sir. He has gone mad, they say."

In spite of himself, the baronet turned pale.

"We meet again!" he gasped, hoarsely, addressing Arthur Maverick. "You have struck me, outraged me: you shall answer with your life."

And seeing that the way was clear, he hastened forth and mounted his horse. A moment afterward, he was going down the avenue at full speed.

Suddenly a hoarse and prolonged bay was heard in the grounds. Then a white object darted swiftly from a mass of shrubbery on his track.

The blood-hound had seen and was pursuing him.

CHAPTER VI.

THE MAD DOG.

THE baronet rode on at the full speed of his horse.

That deep and ominous bay had shown him his danger, and he had now a double reason to fear the blood-hound. Not only was the animal his sworn enemy as the murderer of Giles Maverick,—he was mad, and his bite was mortal, no longer a mere wound.

Thus it was a race for life. As he went on at headlong speed, he heard the hound on his track.

The dog had cleared the tall gate in the wall enclosing the grounds, at one leap; had plainly descried the baronet going at full speed over the high-road; and now, with hanging tongue, quick pants, and grinning mouth, he pursued him at a pace which promised to put his enemy in his power in a few minutes.

Sir Murdaugh Westbrooke was brave, but his heart sank within him as he drove his horse on. The hoarse bay of the mad hound rang in his ears like the trump of doom. Every instant he seemed to be gaining on his enemy in the wild race.

Suddenly his horse, into whose sides he had driven the spur mercilessly, stumbled and half fell.

With a curse, his rider dragged him up, and again struck the spur into him.

But the instant thus lost was nearly fatal to the baronet. The hound reached him and sprung at his throat, his eyes glaring, his mouth slavering.

But for the sudden grasp on the bridle, that moment would have been the baronet's last. The horse rose to his feet again, and the blood-hound missed his spring. The sharp teeth, instead of fixing themselves in the baronet's throat, clutched his riding boot.

Death had grazed him thus, and he improved the incident promptly.

With a blow from his clenched hand, cased in a heavy riding gauntlet, he hurled the hound from him. The animal rolled over on his back, and again the baronet went on headlong, intent on nothing now but escape.

All at once, however, the ominous bay was again heard. With a sudden chill at his heart, he turned his head and looked back. The hound was once more pursuing him, more resolute and enraged than before.

At that spectacle the murderer felt a pang of mortal fear. Despair clutched him, as he felt the venomous teeth would soon do. The image of the man whom he had assassinated rose and " shook his gory locks at him." In the agony of his soul he shouted, —

" Help! help! that dog will murder me. Help!"

Suddenly his horse shied violently. He had nearly ridden over a man in the road. This man was rudely clad, and shouted, —

" What be the matter?"

" The dog!" gasped the baronet.

And he looked over his shoulder.

The mad blood-hound was within ten feet of him.

" Ten guineas if you kill him!" he gasped.

As he spoke, the hound sprung. But the man had understood, and met him.

They clutched and rolled on the road, locked in a mortal hug.

The baronet did not wait. He put spur to his horse and disappeared at headlong speed toward Westbrooke Hall.

He was saved.

———

An hour afterward one of the fraternity of wolves entered Oldport, with his breast covered with blood.

The blood flowed from a deep wound in his throat, which had swelled suddenly.

When his brother wolves questioned him, he said he had met a man chased by a dog, the man had offered him ten guineas to kill the dog, and he had killed him.

Then the "wolf" ceased speaking, and began to snap at those around him.

Two days afterwards he was attacked with convulsions, and four men were required to hold him.

On the next day he was calmer, but suddenly drawing up his limbs, expired.

The dead hound had been discovered on the road to Maverick House. The "wolf" had succeeded in strangling him, but the mortal poison had been communicated.

He had died of the bite of the mad dog, in place of the baronet, and even the ten guineas were unpaid.

CHAPTER VII.

THE BURIAL OF THE WOLF.

THE wolves followed their dead companion to the grave, with solemn ceremony.

The scene of sepulture was a wild spot on the very brink of the sea, and the fishermen had enclosed the space by piling up masses of rock, which from the channel resembled rough defences against cannon.

Up the rugged path which led to this burial place they now bore the dead wolf, the rude coffin enclosing his remains carried on the shoulders of his brethren; and reaching the wall, they lifted the coffin over, and carried it to the side of the grave.

Then the ceremony of interring a member of the fraternity of the wolves began. No priest of any denomination was present, and there was something heathenish in the strange rites.

Hands were joined around the grave, the wolves circled it slowly, beating the ground with monotonous feet; then a wild and melancholy chant rose, and was carried away by the wind.

This lasted for half an hour. Then the hands were unlocked and the coffin lowered into the grave amid deep murmurs.

"Who is this we be a burying?" came in hoarse tones from the gigantic Goliath.

"A wolf!" was the muffled response from the voices of all present.

Goliath extended his hand solemnly.

"So mote it be!" he thundered; "and cursed be the man who moves the bones of a wolf!"

As he spoke he took a handful of earth and threw it on the coffin. The men did likewise, each in turn, and the grave was speedily filled.

Then the wild-looking figures joined hands and encircled the grave once more, beat the ground with their feet, and repeated their monotonous chant.

It ended at last. They left the burial ground, and slowly wound down the hill toward the coast. As they disappeared, night descended, and the moon rose, throwing her pallid light on land and sea.

15

Such had been the wolf's burial.

An hour past midnight, and a figure leaped the wall, followed in a moment by another.

The moon revealed the faces of these men, who carried picks and spades. They were the two rough personages whom Earle and the gypsy had encountered that night bearing the corpse into Westbrooke Hall.

"This is the place, mate," said one of them; "it is easily found."

"By the fresh earth — you are right."

"And now to work; this job is dangerous."

"Dangerous?"

"This is one of the wolves, and I'm told they are sworn to put a knife into whoever disturbs one of 'em."

"Ough! I never heard that."

"It makes the job worth five guineas more."

"Exactly."

And without further words they proceeded vigorously to work.

In an hour the coffin responded to the blow of the pick.

"Take care, mate!" said one, as the dull sound was heard.

"Right."

And proceeding more carefully, they soon

unearthed the long box without noise, and wrenching off the lid, dragged forth the dead body.

"He's a rough-looking one," muttered the man who lifted the corpse, "and his neck is all swollen."

"On account of the dog."

"Hurry up, mate."

And laying the body on the earth, they proceeded rapidly to fill up the grave again.

This was soon accomplished, and they then lifted the body over the fence, and bore it on their shoulders down the rough path leading toward the interior.

In a clump of bushes a small vehicle was waiting. Into this they pushed the corpse as if it were the body of an animal.

"Come on, mate; I don't like this job. Seems . to me they are à watching of us."

And the speaker hastily got into the wagon. The other followed, and in a business-like way took his seat on the corpse.

Then the single horse was whipped up, the vehicle rolled away, and night swallowed it.

The grave of the wolf had been rifled. Would the curse descend?

CHAPTER VIII.

THE CHASE.

IT was the night succeeding these events. Darkness and storm had rushed down simultaneously on the coast of Pembrokeshire.

The surges of St. George's Channel, lashed to fury by the breath of a veritable hurricane, broke in thunder on the jagged reefs and ledges of rock jutting from the water, and died away in the cavernous recesses beneath the great headland near Oldport, like the hoarse bellowing of bulls, or the dull boom of artillery.

The coast was absolutely deserted. Scarce a light glimmered in Oldport. On the headland, no beacon light warned barks off the perilous reef. The light of the blood-red moon alone, shining through a rift in the black clouds, toward the east, contended with the ebon darkness, and revealed, in their full horror, the foam-capped reefs.

All at once a sail-boat might have been seen darting toward land. It was a vessel of the smallest size, and careened terribly under the great pressure of canvas.

Clinging to the single mast was a man wrapped in a dreadnought, and with his hand in his breast. Three other men were on the bark, but they were crouching, pale and sullen.

"We'll all go to the bottom!" said one of the men, who seemed to be the owner of the boat.

"You are paid!" was the gruff reply of Wilde — for he it was who stood erect, clinging to the mast.

"What's pay if we go down?" said the sullen one.

"But we wont!"

"Look at that reef! Down with the helm!"

And he started to his feet.

The vessel grazed a grinning reef, scraped, and darted on. She was a mere cork — the winds drove her like a dry leaf of autumn over the foaming waves.

"If I only arrive," muttered Wilde, "I have my fortune here!"

And he clutched a package in his breast,—the pocket-book containing the stolen leaf from the register at Martigny.

"Look!" suddenly shouted the skipper of the vessel. "There is that devilish craft following us still!"

And he pointed to a sail-boat similar to his own, which was darting towards them.

Wilde uttered a curse.

"I thought you had got away from her!"

"I thought so too! But there she is,—followed us all the way from the coast of France!"

And, knitting his brows, he muttered,—

"A sailor is on board of her! I believe I'll throw this Englishman overboard, and strike to the craft that's been pursuing us!"

Wilde heard the muttered words, and drew a long knife from beneath his coat.

"Death to the man who touches me!" he growled, with the accent and manner of a wild animal.

"And death to the man who is running us on these reefs to go to the bottom!"

As he spoke, the Frenchman drew a knife in

his turn, his companions exactly imitated him, and they rushed straight on Wilde.

It was too late.

Before they had reached him where he stood, clinging with his left hand to the mast, a crash like thunder was heard, the bark staggered, and reeled backward. She had run right on a reef, and two of the Frenchmen were hurled overboard.

As they disappeared, a single cry cut the darkness like a steel blade. An instant afterwards the heads were engulfed and the men dashed to pieces on the jagged rocks.

The third Frenchman uttered a shout of rage, and struck at Wilde.

As he did so, his foot slipped.

An instant afterwards Wilde had seized him and hurled him into the sea.

The craft grated with harsh thunder on the rocks, and then darted ahead.

The momentary arrest of her progress had, however, given her pursuers time to gain upon her.

As she drove on now, the craft following hovered above her, on the summit of a gigantic wave — and in the prow a man, wrapped in a cloak, gazed eagerly toward her.

"She struck, Captain!" said one of the men, "and look!—again!"

In fact, the sail-boat containing Wilde, had rushed straight on a still more dangerous reef.

It finished her. The sharp teeth tore her hull to shreds—she burst in two, and her mast sunk, dragging the sail like the wing of a wounded sea-bird. Wilde was thrown into the water, and struck out powerfully for the strand, now not two hundred yards distant.

"He will escape!" cried the man in the boat in pursuit.

And without a moment's hesitation he threw off his cloak, and plunged into the boiling waves.

Then a tremendous contest took place between the adversaries. On one side was enormous strength and great skill as a a swimmer; on the other, equal skill,- if not so much strength, and a burning resolve to reach the man he was in pursuit of, or die.

The wind howled; the waves struck them; the moon was blotted out; all was darkness. Still Wilde darted on, pursued by Earle.

CHAPTER IX.

WHILE these events were occurring on the storm-lashed coast of St. George's Channel, a sombre scene might have been witnessed at Westbrooke Hall.

In an apartment of the mansion, furnished with only two or three chairs and a long pine table, Sir Murdaugh Westbrooke, clad in his old dressing-gown, with the sleeves rolled up, was dissecting a dead body.

The corpse was that of the "wolf," carried off from the lonely spot near the sea; and at the door stood one of the rough persons who had effected the robbery of the grave, thus providing the "subject" which the baronet was engaged in dissecting.

Sir Murdaugh, with animated movements,

and an expression of horrible avidity in his
eyes, cut away at the body: the man gazed at
him with interest and a curiosity which was
plain in his expression.

All at once the baronet turned, bloody scalpel
in hand, and grinned. His yellow tusks protruded frightfully thereupon, and, to speak
plainly, he was extremely hideous.

"Gubbs!" he said.

The man thus addressed returned, —

"Your honor?"

"This seems a strange way of amusing myself, Gubbs?"

As the words were uttered in the tone of an
inquiry, the man said, —

"Yes, your honor."

The baronet grinned again. The occupation
in which he was engaged always put him in a
good humor. To see the flesh of his dead sub-
jects divide at the application of the knife,
almost invariably communicated a singular
and repulsive cheerfulness to the baronet's
expression.

"You wonder, I suppose, Gubbs," he said,
"why I dissect. Well, suppose I tell you. It
is simple, and easily explained. When I was a
young man, I acquired a taste for surgery in

the great hospitals of Paris. I was poor—was then simple Murdaugh Westbrooke; studied surgery. Afterwards I had no occasion to enter the fraternity of leg and arm cutters; but I was as fond as ever of this—I am fond of it still; and so I amuse myself, you see, Gubbs, in this highly scientific manner."

The tusks became the most prominent features in the baronet's face as he spoke. His yellow teeth came out too, jagged and awry; his eyes, bloodshot but glittering with pleasure, rolled in their cavernous sockets.

"Other men like wine and cards and women," said the baronet, plunging his knife into the body,—"I like this!"

And with a keen stroke, he cut into the subject, making a clear circular incision which nearly divided it.

"Every man to his taste! this is mine."

And he eagerly repeated the stroke. As he did so, the knife slipped, and inflicted a slight wound upon his hand.

"Take care, your honor," said the man, "I've hearn that was dangerous."

"What?"

"To cut yourself while you were carving away at one of them."

And he pointed to the body.

"True, it is sometimes. But a little water will prevent danger."

And going to a basin he washed his hands and looked at it.

The knife had punctured the palm and blood exuded.

"An ugly scratch!" he muttered, "but no harm can come of it now."

As he spoke, he bound a handkerchief around the hand, and returned to his work.

"Anything further to do, to-night, your honor?" said the man.

"Nothing, but come back to-morrow."

All at once hurried steps were heard, and the door was thrown open.

As it flew back, Wilde rushed in; his face flushed, his eyes sparkling, his clothes wet and dripping.

"You have it!" exclaimed the baronet.

"Yes, your honor,—but I am nearly dead. He—that one—pursued me; both boats were wrecked on the reef yonder. I swam ashore, he after me,—he clutched me just as I touched land. I stabbed him, and got off in the dark."

The baronet had scarcely listened.

"The paper!" he exclaimed.

" Here it is, your honor."

And Wilde drew forth the leaf which he had stolen from the register, — the proof of Sir Murdaugh's marriage with Marianne Earle.

CHAPTER X.

THE DEN OF THE WOLF.

WILDE had accurately narrated what had taken place between himself and Earle. The sailor by almost superhuman efforts had succeeded in coming up with his opponent just as Wilde emerged half dead with cold and exhaustion from the blinding surf; had grappled with him, intent alone on arresting his further progress; and the powerful gamekeeper thus assailed by his mortal foe, had just strength enough to draw his knife and strike at Earle as the latter clutched him.

The knife passed through the fleshy part of the sailor's arm, and inflicted a painful wound.

It was far from disabling him however, and it was the darkness alone which saved Wilde.

He tore away from Earle as he struck, pushing back his opponent as he did so; then, with a single bound, he disappeared in the gloom, running rapidly over the sandy shore, which gave back no sound, and enabled him to evade his pursuer.

Earle had rushed after him, but all was in vain. Wilde had vanished, and no sound indicated the direction in which he had gone. In ten minutes the sailor gave up the pursuit, and stopped, panting and nearly exhausted from the blood which he had lost from his wound.

He looked around him. All was dark. A few lights glimmered in the village of Oldport. He dared not venture there in his full uniform of a captain in the French navy; and looking for the bark which had brought him, he could nowhere discover it.

"One thing only is left," he muttered, — "to go to my mother."

And traversing the surge-lashed shore, along the edge of the water, he reached the narrow path running along the ledge of rocks — then that which wound up the preipice to the hut of the recluse.

No one but a sailor, sure-footed and accustoned to work with hands and feet in the dark, could have found his way safely up the dizzy path toward the summit. More than once he passed near the very brink of the precipice; a step out of the pathway, would have hurled him a thousand feet down into the boiling abyss. But he went on safely. No chamois could have traversed the narrow way more rapidly and surely. Soon he reached the last and most dangerous point; passed it; reached the summit, and hastened to the hut of the recluse.

No light was visible. The spot seemed deserted.

Earle struck the door with his clenched hand. It flew open, but within all was darkness and silence.

He entered. A strange sinking of the heart suddenly assailed him. Where was his mother? Why this darkness and silence, instead of her smile and warm greeting?

He went toward the narrow bed, and felt for his mother there. She might be asleep.

The bed was vacant. The cold pillow was round and unpressed.

She was gone!

Earle sat down, faint in body and mind. A sombre foreboding siezed upon him. What was the origin of this absence?

Suddenly he rose with a hoarse cry.

"That man! — that wretch! He has probably murdered her! He has discovered her! He came here, I now remember, in search of me! He sent to France to steal that proof of his marriage! He has secured both obstacles to his new marriage, — the record, and the person of the first wife!"

Earle pressed both hands to his forehead, and staggered.

What should he do?

With weak and uncertain steps, but a wild excitement in his breast, he tottered out of the hut, went toward the precipice, traversed the dizzy brink with the instinct of a blind man, descended the path, reached the shore, then, scarce knowing what he did, he staggered on toward the village.

All at once there rose before him in the darkness a weird-looking object.

It was the hull of a wrecked vessel, turned upward and fitted up as a rude dwelling. A ray of moonlight as red as blood enabled him to make out its surroundings. These were nets, an old anchor, a coil of rope, and an old buoy. The door was a hole scarce large enough for a man to crawl into. It was open now, and Earle saw crouching over a few embers, a gigantic figure.

Something in this figure struck him as familiar. He tottered forward and looked in. The figure raised its head. By the glimmer of the embers Earle recognized Goliath.

The next moment he staggered to the doorway, uttered a low cry, and fell forward into the arms of the chief of the wolves, who had recognized him, and drew him into his rude dwelling, radiant with joy at his return.

"You be come up out of the foam, master!"
Earle tried to reply, but fainted.

CHAPTER XI.

KIDNAPPED.

IN an upper room of Westbrooke Hall, difficult of access, and almost unsuspected, so carefully was it concealed by jutting gables and angles, sat the recluse whom we left in her hut on the headland, when Earle set out for Maverick House.

Two days before, she had been kidnapped. This was very simply effected. The man Gubbs, in the absence of Wilde, the baronet's factotum, undertook the affair, went thither after midnight, simply seized and gagged the solitary woman, forced her to enter a light carriage, and then drove off swiftly through woodland by-roads to Westbrooke Hall, which they reached before daylight.

The recluse was then conducted to the apartment which we have spoken of above ; the door was locked upon her; she was left to her reflections ; and, whilst still engaged in this occupation, Sir Murdaugh had entered.

"Welcome to Westbrooke Hall, your ladyship!" was his ironical greeting. "Can I do aught to render your sojourn here more agreeable ? If the servants exhibit any neglect, pray inform me of the fact, Charmed to see you, my dear madam, — really charmed, upon my word!"

The recluse looked at him coldly. There was not a particle of nervous trepidation in her expression.

"You do not reply, my lady. Pray honor me with a few words: your voice invariably charms me."

"I do not reply because I have none to make, sir," said the woman, with entire calmness. "What response is necessary to an outrage like this?"

"An outrage, madam?"

"Is it not an outrage to send a wretch in your pay to seize an unprotected woman and to drag her off thus to a place of concealment?"

"Well, it *is* irregular."

The baronet grinned and was evidently enjoying himself.

"Your object?"

"Well, shall I be frank with you, madam?"

"If you can."

"Shall I tell you my first plan, or my second?"

"Speak!"

"First, I thought I would—well, would—*murder* you, my dear madam. That is an ugly word, but you may retort that it suits *me*. Perhaps it does. I am not a beauty, and my life, tried by a strictly moral standard, may not be beautiful morally. Yes! I thought I would get rid of you."

"Why have you not done so, then?" was the cold inquiry.

The baronet's face grew dark.

"It is not too late," he said in a threatening tone; "beware how you defy me."

"Defy you? Do you suppose I am afraid of you? No! do as you will. Yes! I do defy you."

And the woman rose to her full height.

"I never feared you," she said, looking at him with superb scorn in her eyes. "I fled from you to rescue a child from your poisonous association.　That child is safe from you now. You cannot harm him, for he knows you.　As to me, what care *I*, think you?　Nothing."

And she sat down again.

The baronet scowled at her with sudden wrath.　Then this changed to a sneer.

"Good, good!" he said; "the same spirit that used to blaze out in Marianne Earle, twenty years ago.　Ah! you look at me with your fine disdain.　You would say that I provoked you then.　Well, so be it; let that go.　I am here to speak of the present and future — *your* future.　I will do so very briefly, madam.　I brought you here intending to get rid of you, if necessary.　It is not necessary.　I will simply send you to St. Domingo.　My good servitor, Wilde, who is known to you, will accompany your ladyship.　He is absent now on important business, but will soon return.　Then I will call on madam again."

And sneering, he went out abruptly.

CHAPTER XII.

MASTER AND MAN.

SUCH were the events which had occurred during the brief absence of Earle and Wilde.

We left the baronet and this latter worthy in the apartment containing the corpse, the eyes of Sir Murdaugh fixed joyfully on the paper which Wilde had brought him.

"At last I have it," he exclaimed. "From this moment I am safe."

Wilde glanced sidewise at the man, Gubbs, and the baronet nodded.

"You can go now," he said to the man, who at once left the apartment.

"And now to business, Wilde," added the baronet. "Much has been done in your absence."

"What, your honor?"

"That woman is here, a prisoner in this house. But, before I speak further of this, tell me all about your journey."

"That I will do in few words, sir."

And Wilde narrated every thing, concluding with the scene which had occurred on the beach.

"That man is an incarnate devil," growled the baronet. "He is ever on my track. Not content with denouncing me as a murderer, he is now here again to thwart and endanger me."

"There is but one thing left your honor," said Wilde in a low tone.

The baronet looked at him intently.

"I understand you — yes," he said.

Compact of murder was never made more clearly in fewer words. But the baronet seemed determined that there should be no doubt whatever.

"That man must die, Wilde; no mincing of words. We have gone too far to recede."

The words were uttered in a whisper.

"The thing is plain, sir," was the reply in the same tone; "while he is alive, you are in danger, to say nothing of *me*. I don't intend to rest. Give your orders, sir. They shall be obeyed."

The baronet sat down, and gazed at the floor.

· "Where is he?" he said suddenly; "since you stabbed him, he must be near Oldport. Was the wound dangerous?"

"Only in the flesh of the arm."

"That is nothing! Act promptly. Go and look for him to-night! This is all the more necessary, as he will come quickly to look for us!"

"I understand, sir."

"*She* is here! He will be on our track, since he must suspect me of the abduction."

Wilde buttoned up his wet coat.

"I will take Gubbs, and hunt him to-night, sir."

"Do so, and return before daylight. Things are hurrying in many ways, Wilde. Listen! I am to be married in eight days. In three days *that woman* must be out of England. If in twenty-four hours *he* is dead we are safe, and you will have earned one thousand pounds. If he lives — the gallows —! I am rich and influential, and may escape. You are poor and nobody — you will hang! Go, now! You may find him in some corner, fainting and weak from loss of blood. You are a man of decision; you will not neglect that chance.

Go, go! His death secures everything. Whilst he lives, — listen, Wilde, — the halter is around your neck!"

"And yours!" muttered the Hercules as he hastened from the apartment.

CHAPTER XIII.

A TIGRESS.

AS Wilde disappeared, the baronet fixed his eyes with avidity upon the paper in his hand.

"The actual entry!" he muttered; "Murdaugh Westbrooke to Marianne Earle, Martigny, April 17 —, signed by Father Ambrose; all in due form! Decidedly, Wilde is a cool hand, and has effected all I hoped for. Now to action! But first to enjoy my little treat!"

He went out quickly, and ascending the broad staircase, took a key from his pocket and opened a door. Before him, in a bare apartment, sat the recluse, pale but calm.

"I have come to call on you, madam," he said, grinning.

The recluse coldly inclined her head.

"I have an interesting communication to make, madam."

The recluse gazed at him intently, but made no reply.

"Your ladyship is silent this evening, but no matter. I will talk myself. And first, I beg to call your ladyship's attention to the fact that this is the record of our marriage in the village of Martigny — brought for my private perusal by our mutual acquaintance, Mr. Wilde."

The baronet watched her closely. At these words she turned suddenly pale.

"Doubtless a copy, sir!" she said, coldly, but with a sudden, eager glance.

The baronet burst out laughing. It was a sombre and ghastly sound..

"A copy? By no means, madam. The original paper! I was too intelligent to care for a copy. I wished to feast my eyes upon the sole and only evidence of our connubial bliss! What cared I for a *copy?* What I wanted was the actual sheet from the record, signed by the priest: here it is; and from this moment there is no proof whatever of our marriage."

The recluse was pale, but her calmness had returned.

"So you are bent on destroying all proof that I am Lady Westbrooke?"

The baronet bowed and said ironically,—

"Madam is intelligent."

"You design marrying again?"

"I do, madam."

"To commit bigamy?"

"There is no bigamy where proof does not exist of a former marriage."

The recluse made no reply. With her eyes fixed intently upon the baronet, she seemed to listen coldly.

"Why make so much ado, my dear madam," he said, with a sombre grin. "Are we so much devoted to each other that we cannot bear to ignore that former union? Was it of hearts — or hands only? I think it was merely the hand. Well, I count that a sin. I design to unite myself now to a young creature who loves me?"

No reply came from the recluse. The baronet went on:—

"Shall I tell you of my little affair? The fair one is called Ellinor Maverick. She is exceedingly handsome — much more handsome, I must say, than *you* ever were; and she marries

me in defiance of the whole respectable Maverick family."

The recluse had never removed her eyes
from the face of the baronet.

" Does she know that you have one wife living ?" she said, calmly.

The words brought to the baronet's face the
eternal grin.

"I must confess she does not, madam!
She is a tender lamb led to the slaughter.   I
am a monster, you perhaps think, and I confess
I am not a saint.   Bnt in this case the lamb is
tough !   Miss Maverick weds me for my estate,
not from the sympathetic impulse of her maiden
heart!   She calculates — she does not gush
out !   I am Sir Ten Thousand a Year, rather
than Sir Murdaugh Westbrooke ; and a few
little charges which have been brought against
me have had no influence on the sweet charmer
— she is still determined to marry me."

"And you will ruin this young woman because she is worldly and ambitious ?"

" Ruin her, madam ? not at all ? How shall
I ruin her ? "

The recluse pointed coldly toward the paper
in his hand.

" Still harping upon this !" the baronet said

with a grin. "I will show you how I remove that little difficulty in the simplest manner, madam?"

He caught the paper with both hands, and was about to tear it in pieces.

"Forbear!" cried the recluse, suddenly rising and confronting him.

"Forbear what?" he growled.

"From the commission of the crime you meditate!" his companion said, with flushed cheeks. "It is your soul's salvation you imperil! I do not speak of the offence against law! Think, unhappy old man!—for you are old now, as I am,—think, God has forbidden this. You sin wilfully against his commandments! Stop now, on the threshold!—repent!—a poor sinner urges that! Abandon this scheme!—remember that your lawful wife still lives!—Give me the paper!"

And before he divined her intention, she grasped the paper and tore it from him.

The baronet uttered an enraged cry and said,—

"Beware!—give me back that writing!"

"It is mine equally—since it is the record of my marriage!" she exclaimed, recoiling, and thrusting the paper into her bosom.

"Give me the writing!"

And he seized her by the wrist, with a grasp of iron.

"Release me, sir!"

"Give me the paper!"

"I will not!"

He seized her by the throat.

"The paper — or you are dead!"

The hand grasped the white throat more furiously.

"Kill me, then!—you may take it from my dead body—I will never surrender it!"

He tore open her dress, and drew the paper from its hiding-place.

"Coward!" she exclaimed, as he did so; "wretch, to outrage me thus!—to lay the hand of violence where you once laid your head! Oh! I could tear the very flesh which was so profaned once!—coward!"

And with flaming eyes she confronted him, —eyes full of superb wrath.

"Insult, outrage, murder me if you will!" she cried, in her rage and scorn. "There is one person who is safe from you — your child!—whom you aimed to murder! unnatural and monstrous! Of what race do you

come? You would. slay your own child!—
but he at least is safe from you!"

The baronet had retreated a step as she confronted him with blazing eyes. In spite of
himself, he shrunk before the scorn of his
companion. Now, however, his sneer returned
— the ghastly grin distorted his ugly mouth.

"Ah! you think that whelp is safe, do you,
madam? You are mistaken. Wilde stabbed
him to-night!"

"You lie — he is in France!"

"I do not lie, madam — he is in Pembrokeshire."

The woman looked at him; as she did so
the flush died out of her cheeks.

"Where is he?"

"I will not tell you!"

She trembled.

"For pity's sake!"

And suddenly submissive she clasped her
hands.

"Do not harm him! He has not wronged
you! Why do you thus hate him?"

"Because he hates *me*, and will destroy me
— if I do not destroy him! Cease your prayers,
then — they are vain! His doom is sealed —
Wilde is now tracking him!"

17

"That wretch? Oh, it is infamous! He will murder him! Let me go and save him!"

The baronet thrust her back violently, and went toward the door.

"It is too late! he is doomed!"

And he reached the door and opened it.

Suddenly the woman threw herself upon him, and seized his throat with both hands.

"Give me my child!" she cried, with the rage of a tigress robbed of her young.

His reply was to hurl her from him, and she fell at full length on the floor. A moment afterwards the baronet had passed through the door and closed and locked it.

As the key turned in the lock, the door shook under the grasp of the poor mother.

"My child! my child! Give me my child!" she moaned, shaking the door.

A laugh replied; and the baronet's footsteps receded. A moment afterwards a body fell heavily in the apartment which he had left.

The recluse had fainted.

CHAPTER XIV.

THE INTRUDER.

SIR MURDAUGH WESTBROOKE descended to his sitting-room.

The grin had disappeared from his lips and there was no longer the former expression of hideous triumph in his eyes.

He sat down, and gazed for fully a quarter of an hour into the, fire, which was dying down now.

"How will this end?" he muttered. "I am knee-deep in blood, and am going in waist-deep! Am I then a wretch unable to withhold myself from crime? Why do I venture on this marriage. Why do I plan that boy's destruction? Is the Devil my prompter? Doubtless, since he has just made me outrage a woman — cut her to the heart — inflict personal violence upon her!"

He knit his brow, and his lips writhed.

"I am a lost soul, I think!"

And he rose to his feet.

"She cowed me yonder to-night when — yes, I was a coward to outrage that bosom! It was Marianne Earle's once — I loved her — have never loved any one else! Yes, yes, I was a coward! And I aim to prove myself a worse coward still!"

He looked at the paper which he held in his hand. "Marianne Earle, Martigny, April 17, ——," seemed burnt in flame upon it.

"She was beautiful then! — the only dream of my life!" he muttered. I loved her — could have died for her — for six months!" he added, with a cruel sneer.

And leaning against the tall carved mantelpiece, he pondered, his face gradually growing dark.

"No! it is too late to recede — and to defy that boy Arthur is delicious! This marriage is necessary — it removes suspicion! It ties their hands, for I will be the husband of Ellinor Maverick, their own blood! Then — then, with this woman and that other enemy gotten rid of

—with no fears any longer, and the failing health of the Viscount Cecil to count on — !"

He slowly tore the paper in pieces and threw it into the fire.

"The die is cast!" he muttered; "my sentimental mood is over! Sentiment for me! I was an innocent man once, now I am what? What have I to do with *sentiment?* Can the wolf that is hunted find time to snivel and wipe his eyes? Away with such imbecility! I am a man again, and will ride over all enemies. Aid me, Devil! if there be a Devil!"

And, with a face distorted into a hideous grin, the baronet took from the table the only light in the apartment, slowly crossed the drawing-room, opened and passed through the door, and then his steps were heard slowly ascending the staircase.

Ten minutes after his disappearance, a slight sound might have been heard at the rear window.

This window opened, as the reader will remember, directly on the park; and for more than a half an hour a man standing on the ledge beneath it had been watching the baronet, his eyes on a level with the window-sill.

As the figure of the baronet disappeared now,

a dusky arm suddenly rose from without. As the arm rose, the moon came out, and revealed a man's head and shoulders above the sill. Then the hand stealthily passed through a broken pane in the window — the bolt was silently shot back — a moment afterwards the sash was raised — and, silent as a shadow, the man stood in the room.

It was the gypsy: his countenance expressed mingled curiosity and apprehension. The swarthy face was plain in a vagrant gleam from the dying fire, and toward the fire he now moved with a cautious and stealthy step.

"That paper! — why did he look at it so closely — and then tear it?" muttered the gypsy. "I see it is not burned — only one of the pieces is destroyed!'

He stooped and raised the fragments, joining them together, and closely scanning them.

"Murdaugh Westbrooke — Marianne Earle; Martigny. Why this is a marriage record!" he murmured. "And to think that the good Sir Murdaugh has already been married!"

He looked again at the paper. The name of the woman seemed to strike him for the first time.

"Marianne Earle!" he said, knitting his

brows, and evidently lost in reflection, "Marianne Earle! Earle!—there is some mystery here!"

And his quick mind went back to his association with the sailor. Twice he had heard Earle repeat his own name,—once when carrying off the viscount, in reply to a question from the nobleman, and again during the interview with Arthur Maverick on the night of his escape.

"Earle!" he muttered; "this baronet married Marianne Earle, then! Who was she? was she related to *him*—my brother of the Rommanye Rye?"

His eyes distended suddenly. The vagabond's enormous acuteness had placed him on the track of the mystery. The woman on the headland was Earle's mother. He had divined that when he went to warn Earle on that last night of his stay in Pembrokeshire.

"Aha! Here is something!" he muttered. "It will pay better even than my knowledge of the murderer of Giles Maverick! I am lucky! I came for the baronet's silver: I find out something far more valuable than silver, I think."

And folding up the pieces of paper, he placed them carefully in his ragged pocket.

Then he looked around warily. There was no silver of any description visible.

"The skinflint!" he muttered, with a grimace; "not to leave a spoon, even, for a poor gypsy!"

With stealthy steps he went toward the door which opened on the hall. Not a sound was heard in the funereal mansion but the measured ticking of an enormous clock, which rose, ghostlike, in the corner of the hall.

"Shall I venture farther? It is dangerous, but I will try it. I may find something," he muttered.

The gypsy placed his foot upon the staircase. In the darkness he had not seen the door leading into the room containing the corpse. The terrible odor, however, filled the air, and for an instant his heart failed him.

"What devilish smell is that?" he murmured. "I had best get out of this place."

He turned to go back, but at that moment a stifled groan reached his ears. It died away, then was repetead, then died away again.

The gypsy was even more curious, by nature, than cautious of his personal safety. The muffled sounds roused his curiosity to the highest pitch.

"Something horrible is going on here!" he said, in a low voice. "Shall I try to find what it means? I can gain the window again in two minutes, and neither Wilde nor his hounds are here to follow me!"

He placed his foot once more on the stair: the solid oak did not creak. The second step was as firm; and, rapid and noiseless as a cat, the gypsy reached the second floor.

As he did so the groans were again heard, apparently from an apartment at the end of a dark side passage. The moonlight half-illu-mined the corridor; he stealthily glided toward the sound.

It grew plainer as he advanced. He reached the door from behind which it issued, and, stooping down, applied his eye to the keyhole in which the key had been left.

What he saw made him hold his breath for a moment.

A woman, clad in a dark dress, was kneeling and praying, with clasped hands, and eyes raised to heaven. A ray of moonlight fell upon her face. The gypsy recognized the mother of Earle.

For a moment his heart stood still. A vague idea of the truth came to him. The woman was a prisoner — Earle's mother. Was she the Marianne Earle of the marriage record?

The gypsy's face flushed hot, and, turning his head, he listened. The stifled groans were only heard as the poor woman prayed.

"Now, or never, if I mean to act as *his* friend!" he said to himself.

And silently unlocking the door, he stood before the woman.

She uttered a low exclamation, and shrunk back as he approached.

"Hush!" he whispered, "I am a friend, — I will take you to your son. Listen! His name is Edmond Earle. It was I who came to warn him, you remember, of the baronet's pursuit of him. I understand all. You are a prisoner here. Come with me and make no noise."

She had listened with a nervous tremor in her frame, but this suddenly ceased.

"Yes, yes, I feel that you are a friend. Let us hasten to leave this place."

"Come, then!"

And the gypsy rapidly led the way from the room to the corridor.

"Make haste now!" he whispered. "The baronet has not yet retired. There is his chamber.   See the glimmer of the light through the keyhole!"

Suddenly the voice of the baronet cried,—

"Who is there?   Who is stirring?"

"Run!   Make haste down the stairs!" exclaimed the gypsy.

And he pushed the woman toward the staircase.

Her foot had scarce touched the top step when Sir Murdaugh Westbrooke's door opened violently.

"Who is there?" he shouted, raising a heavy pistol, cocked and ready.

The gypsy's reply was prompt.   He threw himself upon the baronet and hurled him back, knocking up the weapon just as the report of the pistol rang out.

A moment afterwards he had wrenched it from the baronet, and dealt him a heavy blow in the face.   Then he gained the door at one bound; closed it violently and turned the key in the lock; hastily descended the stairs; and taking the woman by the arm, drew her quickly to the window, through which he assisted her to pass, just as the sleepy and frightened servants rushed in to find the meaning of the pistol-shot.

Once in the park, the gypsy cried, —

"To the woods! to the woods!"

"But my son! where is my son!"

"He is in France."

"God be thanked!" she exclaimed. "Then that wretch wilfully lied! He is safe! Then all is well."

And she followed the gypsy, who hastened on.

In ten minutes the shadows of the forest had swallowed the two figures.

CHAPTER XV.

E left Earle in the den of the chief of
the wolves.

"You be come up out of the foam,
master!" the gigantic Goliath had exclaimed; whereupon, overcome by weakness
from the wound in his arm, and exhaustion,
Earle had fainted.

When he opened his eyes the giant was
bending over and bandaging his arm. He
performed this office with rough tenderness,
and as the young man looked up, said, in guttural tones, —

"You be safe here, master!"

"Ah!" murmured Earle.

"You be French — the flag you run out
when they fired on you told that; but French

or no French, you be a wolf, and you be safe here."

Earle quietly extended his hand 'and grasped the huge paw of the wolf.

"Thanks!" he said. "Yes, I need a refuge, and your help!"

"My help?"

"The help of the wolves, perchance — the whole fraternity. I will tell you more of that."

And rising slowly to his feet, he looked through the low port-hole serving as a window, and said, —

"Is it near daylight, brother?"

The reply of the wolf was, that it was scarce midnight.

"Then I will sleep: wake me at daylight!" said Earle.

And stretching himself before the fire, he fell asleep almost instantly.

The giant gazed at him for some moments with a strange expression of solicitude on his face; sat down on a rough stool, having first hung an old blanket before the door; and soon the nods of his huge head indicated that he too slumbered.

It was long hours after midnight, when all at once the gigantic Goliath stirred and muttered in his sleep. The vague sense of impending peril seemed to render him uneasy.

Suddenly the influence appeared to master him, and he rose quickly, and went to the door.

As he did so, two shadows which had hovered near the port-hole window, shrunk back into the darkness behind the overturned hull, and all was quiet.

Goliath muttered some guttural words, shook his head, and returned to his stool. With a glance at Earle, on whose face the glimmering light of the embers fell, he kicked the brands together, wrapped an old pea-jacket around him, and in a few minutes was nodding, sound asleep, beside his companion.

For half an hour nearly, the silence remained unbroken save by the whistle of the wind, and the long roll of the surf, falling with monotonous beat upon the sands. Then cautious steps might have been heard — two figures emerged from the shadows of the hull, and one of these figures, placing his eye at a crevice, muttered, —

" It is our man ! "

For more than a minute he remained silent and motionless, with his hand extended warningly toward his companion behind him.

Then he drew a pistol from his breast, and directed the muzzle toward Earle.

His companion pulled him back almost violently.

"You will get yourself and me killed!" he said, in a hurried whisper.

"Killed?" said the man, impatiently.

"The wolves will swarm at the sound of your shot!"

And Gubbs—for it was that worthy—looked at Wilde with horror-struck eyes.

"You don't know 'em—the wolves," added Gubbs, in the same hurried whisper. "They sleep with one eye open; and this man is one of them, you know, Wilde."

"Yes, curse him!" growled Wilde, lowering his pistol, "you are right."

Goliath started and rose to his feet.

"I swear I heard something," he cried, drawing a long knife.

The movement was followed by the unmistakable sound of steps retreating rapidly. Goliath rushed from the hut; but only in time to see two shadows disappear behind some bushes.

He darted on their track; reached the bushes, and stopped to listen for a moment—not a sound. The mysterious figures had vanished, and with muttered imprecations Goliath turned back.

He saw Earle coming to meet him.

" What is the matter, brother ? " said the sailor.

In a few words, Goliath informed him of this incident.

Earle reflected with a knit brow, for an instant.

" Those men were sent here to murder me, brother," he said, "but their hearts failed them ; we are safe at present. Now for other matters. Is it near day ? "

The giant pointed to a yellow streak in the east.

Earle nodded.

"Come, then, brother. A sailor's first thought is of his craft. I wish to mount that height yonder, and look out for the sail-boat that brought me last night."

" Right, master ! You be a sailor true. If she be wrecked —"

" I shall see her. If she rode through the storm, I shall see her.'

And he led the way toward the height.

" When that is done, we will talk, brother," he said, walking slowly and painfully. " See, we mount ! we will soon arrive.

And he went on, followed by Goliath, and finally reached the summit of the height.

It was the wild and lonely spot used as a place of sepulture for the dead wolves. The rough wall of piled-up rock was clearly seen in the gray light of dawn; and mounting to the top, Earle gazed out on the channel, from which the mists were slowly rising. As he did so, the sun rose, and the curtain of vapor was swept away as if by enchantment.

The sailor uttered an exclamation.

"Look! there she is, brother; she is making for the coast of France."

In fact the sail-boat, which had brought Earle, known easily by her peculiar rigging, was seen scudding before a fresh breeze in the offing, toward the south.

The gigantic Goliath had heard the exclamation of his companion, but had made no reply.

Earle looked round. Goliath was crouching over the rifled grave of the wolf whom he had assisted in burying.

"What is the matter, brother?" said Earle.

Goliath uttered the growl of a wild animal, and seized a board which protruded from the hastily filled grave.

" This be the matter, master," he muttered in a low and fierce tone.

And exerting his herculean strength, he dragged the entire end of the coffin from the grave. It was empty.

" Look ! " said the wolf. " We buried him, and his grave be robbed."

As he spoke, he bounded toward the wall. A part of the shroud had been torn torn off by a sharp fragment.

" They went this way," he growled.

And following the foot-prints rapidly, he reached the spot where the wagon had waited. Here the footprints stopped, and nothing was left but to follow the marks of the wheels, and the horse's feet.

These led towards Westbrooke Hall, and Goliath was about to hasten in the direction thus indicated, when the hand of Earle was laid on his shoulder, and the sailor said, --

" A moment, brother."

The giant turned impatiently.

" I be on the track — woe, to the man who disturbed a wolf."

" I can help you," said Earle.

" You, master ? "

" By leading you to the body."

"You?"

"My interest is to do so. I myself need the help of the wolves."

"For what, master?"

"To attack Westbrooke Hall, where my mother is a prisoner; to release her at the same moment when you recapture our dead brother's body."

The wolf started back, in astonishment.

"At Westbrooke Hall?" he exclaimed.

"Yes!—my mother, and all that is left of our dead brother, who has been carried off! Come, no time is to be lost! I am a wolf!— I make the signal!—to my help, wolves! to my help!"

"That is enough, master!"

And they hurried down the steep pathway, toward the haunts of the wolves.

CHAPTER XVI.

THE ATTACK OF THE WOLVES.

AT an hour past noon on the same day
which witnessed the discovery of the
rifled grave, a singular scene took place
at Westbrooke Hall.

Sir Murdaugh Westbrooke was pacing up
and down his library, with hurried steps, — his
face bruised, and swollen, his eyes glaring with
rage, when suddenly there came to his ears a
strange sound from the park without, — the
sound of furious shouts, hurrying feet, and that
muffled and threatening hum, which rises from
a mass of men bent upon mischief.

At that sound, the baronet suddenly stopped,
and turned his head.

"What is that?" he muttered, with an expression of rage and apprehension mingled.

He hastened to the window. The spectacle which saluted him made him recoil.

In front of the hall was a confused and furious crowd of outlandish figures, — ragged, with glaring eyes, fierce grins, brandished arms, — who were hurrying towards the great door, shouting ferociously as they came ; and in front of them, beside the enormous Goliath, who led the attack, the baronet recognized the pale face of Earle, who wore his full uniform.

" What devil has brought these wretches to attack and perhaps sack my house ? " cried the baronet.

Suddenly his face grew pale.

" Has *she* found him and told him all, and has he come to murder me ? "

He rushed to the door, and violently called out, —

" Wilde ! "

The man had his hand on the door as the baronet opened it. He was trembling.

" Mount and ride to the revenue station, Wilde ! Say I am attacked by these assassins — the wolves ! Kill my best horse, if neccessary ! Ride, and come back with the guard at a gallop ! "

Wilde ran from the library, and disappeared

at a side door. The baronet hastened to the front door of the mansion, where a loud knocking was heard.

"Open!" cried twenty voices.

And the door shook under the pressure of huge shoulders.

The baronet replied by drawing a massive chain across the door, and dropping a heavy bar. The door was already locked — it was thus triply guarded.

"Open!" howled the wolves.

"Who are you?" cried the baronet.

"Open the door! or —"

A tremendous rush was made at the oak.

"I warn you to desist!" shouted the baronet, in a hoarse and trembling voice. "Who comes to invade the privacy — and violate the —"

A howl drowned the rest of the sentence.

"I am a magistrate!"

"Open!"

"This is a felony!"

The door cracked.

"I have sent for the revenue guard. Beware! Disperse, before they charge and fire on you!"

As he spoke, the wolves, in one huge mass

of shoulders, backs, and arms, rushed against
the door.

It gave way, the bar snapped, the chain was
torn from its fastenings, the lock was shattered;
in a moment the wolves had poured in, irresist-
ible as a surge of the ocean, and furious voices
shouted, —

"Our brother! where is the wolf, our
brother!"

Sir Murdaugh Westbrooke, staggered back,
as pale as death and trembling in every limb.

"The meaning of this violence?" he muttered.   "Who is your brother?"

A howl answered him.

He looked round, expecting every moment to
be torn to pieces. His eye fell upon Earle,
who, pale and still, was looking at him.

"You too!" gasped the baronet, — "what
brings *you?*"

"Where is my mother?"

The baronet grew livid, and made no reply.

"Where is my mother, and the record of her
marriage which you had stolen at Martigny?"

The young man's face suddenly flushed.
Rage was gaining the mastery with him.

"I know nothing of her, or the record!"

Earle's teeth were heard grinding together.

" Where is my mother, and that paper ? " he exclaimed, advancing as though about to throttle the baronet. " Answer!   Dare to trifle with me, and, by heaven! though you be my father, I will slay you as I would slay a venemous reptile ! "

The baronet shrunk back, pale and trembling.

At the same instant, a tremendous shout was heard.   It issued from the side apartment, where the wolves had discovered the corpse, and they were seen now, pouring out, the corpse, in its shroud, borne on their brawny shoulders.

" Death ! death ! " they cried hoarsely.

And they rushed on the baronet.

As he staggered back, a loud shout was heard without, and the clash of hooves.

" They are coming !, if I can gain a few minutes ! " muttered the baronet, as pale as death.

And recoiling from the mad crowd, —

" Beware how you outrage a magistrate ! " he gasped.

The hoof-strokes came on like thunder, and men were heard leaping to the ground.

" Wilde has met a party going the rounds : I am saved ! "

And the baronet broke from his enemies.

As he did so, a party of the revenue guard entered the great doorway, with drawn pistols. At their head, tall and commanding, advanced the Viscount Cecil.

CHAPTER XVII.

THE NEWS FROM FRANCE.

THE viscount entered the hall slowly, and his calm eyes surveyed the confused mass of wolves, without apparent emotion.

"What is the meaning of this outrage?" he said; "and that corpse there — what does this mean?"

The baronet hastened toward his kinsman.

"It means that I am attacked and outraged, as you were here, once; and that wretch takes part again in the attack."

The viscount turned suddenly; at sight of Earle he could not conceal his surprise.

"You, sir!" he said; "is it possible that *you* are here and thus engaged?"

"It is possible, my lord, since you see me," returned Earle, in a gloomy voice; "and as to my errand, I am not ashamed of it — a matter I will explain to your lordship."

"It is well, sir," returned the viscount, in a freezing tone. "Wonders never are to cease, then; and life is a play! I leave you in France, and come to England; am riding out, and meet a guard going to protect this gentleman, and take command of it; I reach the scene of the outrage, and lo!—the Baron Delamere commands the insurgents — the terrible mob!"

There was an imperceptible shade of irony, in the nobleman's tones. One thing at least was plain — the outrage to the baronet did not violently enrage him.

" And now a truce to all this," he said. " The cause of this outbreak? Why are these men here ?"

" I will explain in one word, my lord!" said Earle.

And he narrated every thing, connected with the robbery of the grave.

" Your lordship understands now," he added, " why these men are enraged. Sir Murdaugh Westbrooke has violated one of their most deeply rooted prejudices. They look upon one of their fraternity, when dead, as sacred. Sir Murdaugh Westbrooke has violated the grave of one of them, and the wolves rescue their dead brother, my lord!"

The viscount coldly inclined his head.

" And the wolves are right!" he replied.

He turned round to the guard.

" Put up your weapons, and mount your horses."

Then turning to the wolves, —

" Go home with your dead brother," he said. " You know me, and will not disobey me. Rebury that body. If I have power in Pembrokeshire, no others shall be thus outraged."

A hoarse murmur rose from the wolves; but it was plain that they did not design resistance. In fact the Viscount Cecil was as popular with them as Sir Murdaugh was unpopular; and at the word of the high dignitary and manorial lord they bowed their heads in submission.

Goliath went out first, and as he passed before the viscount, doffed his seal-skin cap, and said,—

" You be right, my lord."

" Go, and cease these outrages, Goliath. You are the master!"

Goliath went out, overwhelmed with pride at this recognition.

"Come on, there!" he growled to the fierce water-dogs, who were muttering hoarsely.

At the word from their chief, they moved toward the door. On their shoulders they bore the corpse, and as the heavy feet struck the floor, the monotonous chant of the burial service rose.

Then the wolves, no longer a mob, but in solemn procession, left Westbrooke Hall.

Earle alone remained; his arms folded, his face pale and stern. He was clad in his full uniform, and as the baronet glanced at it, his swollen face was full of satisfaction.

"Well, the insurrection is quelled; the mob has dispersed!" said the Viscount Cecil, with covert irony. "Pray what do you propose further, my good Sir Murdaugh Westbrooke?"

The baronet bounded with rage nearly, at the ill-suppressed satire of the speaker's tones.

"I propose to arrest this person as a French spy, and have him hanged!" he shouted.

"Arrest whom?"

"That wretch!"

And he pointed with a furious gesture at Earle.

"Ah! The Baron Delamere! And as a French spy, do you say?"

"As a spy! whoever he may be."

"You cannot, my dear Sir Murdaugh Westbrooke."

" Cannot ? "

" For the very simplest reason in the world. Spies ply their trade only when two countries are at war. Now France and England have agreed on the preliminaries of a treaty of peace, hostilities are at an end ; and Monsieur le Baron Delamere, there, is on a visit simply to Wales."

He turned and bowed to Earle.

" When in France, I offered you the hospitalities of Wentworth Castle, Monsieur le Baron," he said: " I beg you will do me the honor, now, to accept them."

Earle bowed low, but shook his head. His lips moved; he seemed vainly attempting to speak.

" What is the matter ? " exclaimed the viscount, for the young man had grown suddenly white.

" Thanks, my lord," came from the sailor, in a low weak voice; " but I came hither to — I must — "

He tottered.

The viscount hastened to him, and caught him as he was falling.

" My mother ! That paper ! "

· And letting his head fall on his shoulder, suffused with blood, Earle lost consciousness.

Fifteen minutes afterwards he was in the Viscount Cecil's chariot, which was rolling towards Wentworth Castle. The viscount had been riding out in it, when he met the party of guards, and had directed it to follow; he himself mounting the horse of one of his outriders.

As Earle fainted, he bore him out. They entered the chariot, and it went on its way.

Between the viscount and the baronet not a single word had been exchanged.

So the strange scene ended.

CHAPTER XVIII.

THE CRISIS.

NO sooner had the chariot disappeared with the viscount and Earle, than Sir Murdaugh Westbrooke fell into a chair, and called, in a hoarse and broken voice, —

" Wilde ! "

The Hercules hastened to his master. He had kept in the background hitherto, but now appeared, like a bird of ill-omen swooping down on the field of conflict after the departure of the combatants.

" Wilde ! " the baronet exclaimed, " we must go to work; not a moment must be lost now. Where is that woman ? "

" She must be in the woods somewhere, with that gypsy rascal, your honor," growled the Hercules.

"Search for her instantly, with Gubbs; she must be recaptured before she gives the alarm."

"Yes, your honor."

"Then to work; all is ready. In your absence every arrangement has been made. At the port of Roche, two or three leagues down the coast, the bark *Fly-by-Night* is moored, and the captain is in my pay. He will sail for St. Domingo, as soon as his *passenger* arrives. You understand? He is paid five hundred pounds to conduct a *mad woman* to St. Domingo. The money will close his ears, her ravings will pass unheeded. You will go with her, and see her beyond seas, when you will return and make your report to me. A thousand pounds will await you. Do you understand all now?"

Wilde flushed with joy and cupidity.

"Yes, your honor; at your honor's orders."

"But first to find her! to find her! That cursed gypsy has overturned all my plans. Two things are necessary now, Wilde; let me talk plainly; no ceremony is necessary with you. In a few days I am to be married, but before that day two things must be accomplished. This woman must be out of the country, and that man Earle must be—"

He stopped and looked at Wilde significantly.

The eyes of master and man met. Their glances were dark and meaning.

"Yes, your honor."

"He knows all; can send me and you to the gallows. She is the other obstacle: she can interpose, and forbid the bans on my marriage day. One course only is left. She must be sent away, and he — well, one thing only will silence *him*."

And in a low voice he added, —

"You understand?"

"I understand," growled Wilde. "The woman first; that is the pressing thing."

"Yes: go, now. Take the wagon. Find her, and send her to the ship with Gubbs. Then return here; I will give you my further orders."

Wilde grunted obedience and hurried from the room.

"Things are hastening," muttered the baronet, "and all depends on prompt action. That cursed dead body that brought about all this discovery, that led the wolves to attack me, and brought the viscount here, — would it had been sunk fathoms deep in the waters of the channel, ere I meddled with it. And then this cut? Is there no danger?"

He looked at his hand, punctured by the knife

during the process of dissection.   It was swollen, and he had bandaged it carefully.

"No: it is a trifle.   I have more important matters to think of," he said.

And rising, he paced to and fro, his brows knit, his lips muttering.

"Well, all is touch and go now.   A short time will decide all.   If I can get *her* out of the country, and close *his* lips forever, then safety, security, a bonny bride, and triumph over my enemies.   If I fail — but I'll not think of that; the thought is too horrible!   Now to make my toilet carefully and repair to lady Worsham's.   There my beautiful young bride awaits impatiently her devoted lover."

A sneer passed over his lips, and the yellow tusks were thrust out.

A moment afterwards he had left the apartment.

CHAPTER XIX.

THE PATH TO WENTWORTH CASTLE.

THE chariot containing Earle and the viscount rolled on toward Wentworth Castle, a great feudal pile crowning an eminence above the channel, a few miles south of Oldport.

The scene through which they passed was wild and full of majestic beauty. Dense forests covered the slopes of the great headlands to the right, and from the wall of dark evergreens on their left issued a mountain torrent, which rushed with a sound like thunder beneath a stone bridge which spanned the gulf beneath.

As the chariot reached this point, the castle was seen near at hand, raising its mighty walls above the foliage of its oaks. It was one of these old feudal piles like Caernarvon or Dalbardon, which render Wales so attractive in the eyes of the historical antiquary. All around it brought back the past and excited the imagination, Even weak and burnt up with fever as he was, Earle seemed deeply impressed with the scene.

"I see you are struck with my old castle," said the viscount; "and it is a true relic of antiquity. Edward I. spent a night here, and his son, Edward II., came near being born here instead of at Caernarvon. Even this stone bridge over the torrent dates back two hundred years."

Earl murmured something that was inaudible.

The viscount gazed at his pale face with attention. The dreamy eyes of the young man surveyed the bridge, the torrent, a path leading to it from the forest, and suddenly he said, in a low voice, with a strange and startled look, —

"I have been here before!"

The baronet looked at him curiously.

"You? Well that is possible, sir. But doubtless you recall the occasion?"

"I do not," murmured Earle; "it is strange. But all is familiar to me."

He gazed around him with profound astonishment depicted upon his flushed face.

"That path! I know that path. Stay, my lord: there is a stone cross in the wood yonder."

And he pointed up the steep path.

"True! What does this mean?" muttered the viscount.

"I know not, my lord."

"There is the cross! See, through the foliage. It is built above a well in the forest."

"The Hart's Well?"

The nobleman started.

"You astound me! Then you have really been here in the grounds of Wentworth Castle?"

"I know not. I am in a dream," murmured Earle. "Is there a previous existence? I do not believe it; but all here is familiar. I seem to have traversed that path but yesterday, and to have heard some one utter that name—the 'Hart's Well.'"

He stopped, looking with amazement around him.

"Let us alight, if it please you, my lord."

"Alight?"

"I would ascend that path, and approach the figure in stone of an armed knight through the double row of evergreens!"

The viscount gazed at the speaker with unbounded astonishment.

"The stone figure of the armed knight! the double row of evergreens!" he said, — "then you have visited my house before. What mystery is concealed under all this, sir?"

The nobleman's tones had grown cold and formal. Was this unknown Frenchman some charlatan, then? Had he acted a part in pretending that he had never visited Pembrokeshire before this autumn?

"Truly, something deeply mysterious, to myself, at least, is under this strange recognition," murmured Earle; "but will your lordship permit me to walk? I am strong enough, I think. If my strength fails me, I will sit down and rest on the granite seat, with the Wentworth arms cut in the stone back of the bench."

The viscount gazed at him without speaking. Then he muttered, —

"I will discover the meaning of this!"

Without further words, he stopped the coach, and directed the watchman to proceed to the castle by the main carriage road. With Earle, he struck into the path, supporting the young man, who walked with difficulty, looking around him with strange curiosity as he advanced.

Half-way up the height they came to a fountain surmounted by a cross.

" Here is the well I have often drunk from," murmured Earle, pale and faint.

And he walked on, with the same dreamy and vacant expression in his eyes.

All at once the viscount felt him stagger.

" You are faint !" he exclaimed.

" It is — nothing, my lord. Let us go on. If I am weary, I will rest on the stone bench. See, it is yonder, with the Wentworth arms."

And he tottered forward to the broad seat, upon which he fell, half exhausted.

The viscount no longer said anything. Surprise seemed to have rendered him speechless.

Earle rose after resting for some moments.

" I am — weak — to-day. My wound has drained my blood, he murmured. " But we will soon reach home now ; there are the two rows of evergreens. And look, there is the armed knight ; the stone is discolored since I was here last."

He went on, unaware that the viscount guided his steps, and kept him from falling.

" The old firs ! How well I remember them. There is the one that had an eagle's nest in it !"

The viscount was speechless. The sailor was recalling things which he himself remembered clearly.

They passed through the double row of ever-greens toward the huge pile.

"Here is the knight! One of his spurs used to be broken, and I found and played with it one day!"

The viscount turned pale, and glanced at the statue, which rose from a massive block of granite, in a grass-plat. One of the spurs had been broken off — he had never observed it before.

He looked at Earle with distended eyes. Something strange seemed going on in the young man.

"Why, there is home!" he exclaimed; "one half the great door is open, as always! Is the picture grasping the battle-axe, hanging on the right of the door? And the lady with the blue mantle nearly opposite — is she there? And the fountain, in the small court, with the water spouting from the tritons?"

Earle staggered, and a mist seemed to pass before his eyes. He turned faintly toward the viscount.

"What — does — this — mean? Where am I? Why, this is home! — home! — home!"

And he fainted in the arms of the viscount, who was near fainting in his turn.

CHAPTER XX.

WHAT THE GYPSY WOMAN HAD SEEN.

IT was not until the next night that Wilde made his reappearance.

He then entered the library where Sir Murdaugh was feverishly pacing up and down; and from the haggard appearance of the man's face, and his jaded expression, it was plain that he had just undergone great fatigue.

The baronet stopped and turned around eagerly.

"Well?" he exclaimed.

" I have caught her at last, your honor ! "

"Good ! where is she ? "

"On her way to the coast in the wagon with Gubbs."

The baronet uttered an exclamation of satisfaction.

"That is well!" he said.

Wilde made no reply. The baronet glanced at him. He was gloomy and dispirited.

"What is the matter? Has anything occured? Where did you find her? Has anything taken place?"

"Something unlucky enough, your honor. I will begin and tell you every thing. I followed their steps — her, and that gypsy scoundrel, in the woods, till I lost them. Gubbs was as much at fault as I was ; but we inquired of an old woodman, got on the trail of the gypsies, who have been camping about in the woods, and found 'em at last in the big forest behind Maverick House, where they have been laying low, to keep out of the way."

"Make haste! Come to the point!" cried the baronet, impatiently.

"In a minute, your honor. Well, we came on 'em at last. I heard 'em, and crawled through the brush till I got a sight of 'em, there close to me. An old hag in a red cloak was watching a pot boiling over a fire on two forked sticks; and that gypsy scoundrel was talking to her, while *she* — the woman we were after — was listening. As I got to my hiding-place, I heard the old hag call my name; the next thing she said was that she could get you and me into trouble, and then that gypsy dog, who can never rest till he finds out every thing, plied her with questions till she let out —"

Wilde stopped.

"Let out what? Speak!" exclaimed the baronet, wrathfully.

"What she had seen near the bridge leading to Wentworth Castle twenty years ago!" said Wilde, sullenly.

The baronet turned pale.

"She saw you?"

"Yes, your honor. How could I help that? I had my orders from you, and obeyed 'em! and now I am to get into trouble."

"Cease that growling! She saw — "

"Well, she saw me steal the child of Viscount Cecil!" said Wilde, — "the son of his wife who died twenty years ago."

The baronet gnawed his lip, and his face grew livid.

"You paid me to do it, and I lurked round the castle till I did it," growled the Hercules. "I saw the child come tottering down the path to the bridge, to look at the water. How he came to stray away from his nurse I never knew; but he was there, and I caught hold of him, and lifted him on my black horse, and made through the woods at a gallop, carrying him before me!"

"And — this hag — !"

"Saw me! She was prowling in the brush to steal fowls or any thing. I nearly rode over her, and knew she had seen me. I ought to have killed her, but blood is dangerous! I paid her ten guineas, and afterwards ten more when she met me and knew me for the man that stole the child! Then she went away, and I thought she was dead. I had carried the child to France, — you were at Martigny — and I saw no more of her. Now she has told that gypsy and that woman the whole, — that the Viscount Cecil's child was not drowned in the torrent as all thought, but carried off by me. They know that he lives — is Edmond Earle!"

The baronet drew a long, deep breath. Something seemed crushing his breast.

"Well," he said, "what followed?"

"Why, Gubbs came up, and we jumped into 'em!" was the reply. "I knocked the gypsy rascal on the head, and Gubbs seized hold of the woman. He dragged her off then, and put her in the wagon, where she was gagged, and is now on her way to the *Fly-by-Night*."

"That, at least, is gained," muttered the baronet; "and now for the other part. No one will believe the charge of -that old gypsy hag that I stole a child; many will believe Edmond, son of the Viscount Cecil, when he brands me as a murderer!"

He stopped. The sound of horses' hoofs was heard without.

"He must die! How to compass that!" said the baronet, in a low voice.

As he spoke, steps approached, the door opened, and Earle entered, pale and tottering. ·

CHAPTER XXI.

THE LOVE OF AN OLD MAN FOR A GIRL.

TO explain the young man's presence at Westbrooke Hall, it will be necessary to return to Wentworth Castle for a brief space.

Earle had fainted in the arms of the Viscount Cecil, as we have seen, and it was only with the assistance of several servants, who ran out, that he was borne into the castle.

The viscount, pale and lost in wonder at the strange scene he had witnessed, saw to all his wants, and a sound night's rest seemed to restore the young man to his senses.

He descended on the next morning and managed to swallow a little food, but it was plain that he was laboring under fever. The viscount endeavored to prevail on him to go to his chamber and lie down, but he refused, and in the midst of his host's urging, a carriage drove up to the door, from which descended Arthur Maverick and his sister Rose.

Rose entered, pale and pensive, and the viscount hastened forward to greet her.

"My dear child!" he said,—"and you must permit your old cousin to thus address you!— what has become of your roses? Your appearance distresses me!"

Rose smiled. All at once she saw Earle and turned crimson.

"You, sir,—you here!" she faltered.

The young man bowed, and his face flushed too.

"You did not know that my poor face would meet your eyes here, ·Miss Maverick?"

"No, sir; but I rejoice to see you—"

There she stopped with a deep blush.

"And I to see you again," he said, in a low tone, with much emotion. "I remember that night—what you said—have thought of it often! On the ocean—in my hours of musing —in France, and everywhere, I have seen your beautiful face and heard your voice!"

The young girl blushed crimson. The viscount, busy in greeting Arthur, had heard nothing. Now he turned and saw Rose and Earle conversing like old friends.

"You know my friend, then, the Baron Delamere, my dear Rose!" he exclaimed.

"Very well, cousin — that is — yes, we know Mr. Delamere."

"And are glad to call him our friend," said Arthur, cordially pressing his hand.

Turning to the viscount as he spoke, he explained how their acquaintance had taken place.

"You saved Rose, then," said the viscount to Earle, with deep emotion. "For that alone you deserve and have my gratitude — my very profound gratitude, sir. This young lady is my cousin, and all I love upon earth very nearly. My life has been sad, sir, — her smiles have brightened it. She would live here at Wentworth Castle, as its mistress, after my death, if I could compass that. I cannot. This property goes to a personage very distasteful to me, Sir Murdaugh Westbrooke. Thus, my very dear Rose," he said, turning with a tender smile toward the girl, "you will remain poor in comparison with what you would be, had I my will! And now, the news! I am just from France, you know! How is Miss Ellinor Maverick?"

And the viscount suddenly cooled.

"That young lady is not a favorite with me, to be frank; but she is your relative, Arthur," he added.

"I am sorry for it," said the young man.

And he narrated every thing relating to the young lady, winding up with the statement that in three or four days she was to be married to Sir Murdaugh Westbrooke.

The viscount knit his brows.

"I had heard something of this! But so soon! Then *she*, instead of Rose, will be mistress here!"

All eyes were directed toward the viscount with surprise.

"You do not know the tenor of Lord Wentworth's will, I see," he said, gloomily. "In case of my death without issue, Sir Murdaugh Westbrooke inherits my estate, as, in the case of his death without issue, I would inherit his. Well, my child," he said to Rose, "he is about to marry, and is younger than I am. Thus he and his children will possess this castle after my death. I attempted to secure you one-half, in consideration of relinquishing to the baronet the other half now. He refused. There all ends. Would to God my poor son had —"

He stopped suddenly.

"Your son, sir?" said Earle, looking at him.

"I had a son. I have been married, sir. Lady Cecil died early, and my poor child/ strayed away and was drowned. We followed his footprints to that torrent yonder, and he was never more heard of. But this is sorrowful, — let me try not to cloud your smiles, my dear Rose."

As he spoke a servant entered, and presented a note on a silver salver.

The viscount looked at it, and an expression of vexation came to his face.

"A meeting of magistrates on a matter of importance. My presence is indispensable," he said. "But you will stay and dine with me, my dear Rose and Arthur."

"I regret to say 'tis impossible, my lord. You will come soon to see us."

"Very soon; but remain and entertain my friend, the Baron Delamere. I beg you to do so. You are my own family."

And, with a courteous smile, the viscount took his departure.

Rose and Arthur remained until evening. With every passing moment, Earle found himself gazing with deeper tenderness on the beautiful girl. His wild passion for Ellinor seemed to have merely smoothed the way for this new emotion, as profound and durable as the first was transient, as serenely tender as the former was passionate.

For the first time Earle felt that he loved indeed; and when at last the young lady rose, and took her departure with her brother, Earle felt as though the sunlight had suddenly disappeared from the earth with her smile and the light of her eyes. He fell back into despondency.

The coach, containing Arthur and Rose, rolled away just as night descended upon Wentworth Castle.

The viscount had not yet returned, and Earle sat down, gloomy and lonely. Then all the violent passions, which the presence of the girl had banished, began to tear him once more. He rose and paced the floor, burnt up by the one thought of his mother. Finally a fever seized him; he felt as though his head were burning, and going to a bell, rang it violently.

A servant hastened in.

"My horse!" said Earle, feverishly.

The servant hesited, looking with astonishment at his flushed face.

"Well, my horse! My horse, I say! Saddle my horse, without delay!"

The servant bowed and went out, reduced to submission by the authoritative voice.

Earle then coolly descended, put on his hat and gloves, and went to the great door.

A horse, saddled and bridled, already awaited him. At Wentworth Castle the master never waited.

"Inform the viscount that I have gone out to take a short ride," he said, getting into the saddle.

And leaving the groom gazing with amazement on his agitated face, like the first servant, Earle rode down the great avenue, and, crossing the bridge, went straight on.

What was his destination? He scarce knew. His brain was reeling, and he was burnt up by fever. Only a vague sensation of rage and thirst for revenge upon the baronet possessed him. His mother — that paper — Sir Murdaugh Westbrooke — such were the thoughts that flitted through his weak brain. And setting spur to his horse, he rode toward Westbrooke Hall.

The animal broke into a gallop, and it was a miracle almost that Earle kept his seat as the horse sped on through the darkness. He tottered from side to side, his eyes half-closed, his bosom heaving. With heated brain and burning cheeks, which only rendered more shocking and terrible his death-like pallor, he went on at at full speed, clinging to his animal rather by the instinct of excellent horsemanship than any thing else; — and so, feeble, reeling, fever-stricken, out of his senses nearly, reached Westbrooke Hall, and stood before Sir Murdaugh Westbrooke the moment after he had uttered the words in reference to Earle, —

"He must die!"

CHAPTER XXII.

THE BLUDGEON AND THE ROPE.

AT sight of Earle, the baronet recoiled and shook in every limb. Then a diabolical joy shone in his bloodshot eyes, and his mouth slowly expanded into the hideous grin which was habitual with him.

For a moment, neither of the adversaries spoke. The baronet looked keenly at his intended victim.

Earle was as thin as a ghost, and frightfully pale, except in the centre of his cheeks. There a hectic flush burned, like a red-hot coal. As he had advanced he had staggered. As he looked at the baronet now, his eyes showed plainly that the young man was approaching a paroxysm of fever; that the wound inflicted by

Wilde had at last worked its results, and strength of mind and body were leaving him together.

The expression of diabolical joy in the baronet's face deepened. But, spite of this feeling, the face of Earle seemed to cow him.

"What is — your pleasure?" he stammered. "What brings you to this house?"

"To slay you, if necessary, as you slew Giles Maverick!" shouted Earle, "unless you tell me where I may find my mother!"

The baronet recoiled.

"My mother!" shouted Earle, his hand going to his empty belt, "or, by heaven, I'll have your blood, were you fifty times my father!"

"Then he does not know yet!" came in low, muttered tones from the baronet, as, with his eyes on the young man's hot face, he retreated toward the right-hand apartment.

"My mother! — where is my mother? — and that marriage-record you stole at Martigny?"

As he spoke in his hoarse voice, strident and metallic from the effect of fever, Earle advanced on the baronet, who continued to retreat before him.

In the baronet's eyes there was something frightful, — a venom which may be seen in the eyes of the cobra, when he raises his deadly crest and is about to spring.

" Your mother? I know nothing of her," he said, watching Earle warily, and continuing to retire.

" Murderer! No! You shall not escape me! You are my father, but — "

He staggered. But for the table which stood near him, he would have fallen to the earth. He leaned upon it, and passed his other hand over his brow as though to clear his vision.

" My mother! " he murmured, faintly.

His doom had, in that moment, been pronounced.

The baronet had turned and whispered a few hurried words to Wilde. The latter had disappeared at one bound.

Suddenly Earle seemed to recover his strength, as though by a miracle. On the wall hung a sword. He caught it down and rushed on the baronet.

" Speak! Tell me where to find my mother and that paper," he shouted, " or I will tear you in pieces, whether you be my father or not! Answer, monster that you are, where have you hidden my mother? You murdered Giles Maverick — the very dog who saw it rose to convict you! You robbed the register at Martigny like a felon and a thief! Last, my mother disappears — you may have murdered her, as you would murder me if you dared!"

"I dare!" came in a deep and sombre voice from the baronet.

As he spoke the door of the secret closet in the wall flew open: the figure of Wilde appeared in the opening like a hideous picture in its frame; a bludgeon rose, descended, and fell upon Earle's right temple, and he fell forward at full length, deprived of consciousness, it seemed of life.

"Now for the rope! the rope!" shouted the baronet, hoarsely.

Wilde rushed into the apartment, and threw a rope around the young man's shoulders. Then, at a signal from the baronet, he wrapped and re-wrapped his arms, thus rendering him entirely powerless, even if he recovered his senses.

"What next, sir?" growled the Hercules, breathing heavily, and gazing with knit brows on the prostrate figure.

"Death!" came in a low tone from the baronet, whose face resembled that of a corpse. "Death! He has forced this on me! Death!

and death in presence of the dust of Giles Maverick!"

The Hercules started and turned pale. Rough and unscrupulous as he was, the words of the baronet horrified him.

"You don't mean —"

"Yes," came in the same low voice from the lips of Sir Murdaugh Westbrooke. "What is the difference? It must not take place here! He must be lost sight of, or you and I mount the gallows! He must die that I may live! He shall not first put the rope around my neck, and then, as the son of the Viscount Cecil, inherit this estate! He shall die, and — yonder! He has made himself the champion of Giles Maverick! Let him wake to find himself close to him in the vault! Say nothing! I have resolved on it! Refuse to aid me, and you hang! Two horses! — quick! and tools to open the Maverick vault! Once shut up there, he will not trouble us! — the dead tell no tales!"

CHAPTER XXIII.

AN hour afterwards, a strange, and terrible scene took place at Llangollen church-yard, — a wild and secluded spot in the hills, a league from Westbrooke Hall. The church, ancient and weather-beaten, rose in the midst of a ghostly array of tomb-stones; and the shadows of the sombre evergreens growing thickly along the rude stone wall around the grounds, danced fantastically, as a chill wind agitated their boughs, and sobbed onward.

It was a weird and lugubrious night. The moon was sailing through long streaks of ebon clouds, reaching from horizon to horizon. At one instant the lonely edifice, and the tombs around it came out with sudden brilliance.

Then the moon disappeared and all was wrapped in gloom again, a gloom which the sobbing wind rendered ghastly and funereal.

All at once, as the moon soared forth, lighting up the sombre tombstones and family vaults, — for Llangollen was the place of sepulture for the gentry of the neighborhood, — two figures, carrying between them something which they half supported and half dragged, got over the wall, and rapidly approached a huge stone set in the side of a knoll. This stone was evidently the door to a large vault, and was secured by an iron fastening. Over it, cut in rude letters on the coping was the single word —

" Maverick."

The figures came on rapidly with their burden, which, silent and insensible, resembled a dead body.

" It is here," said one of the men. " Where are the tools? Wrench off the fastening."

The other obeyed the order, and, inserting an instrument, succeeded in forcing the vault.

" Open !" came from the other.

A huge shoulder was placed against the stone and it slowly revolved, grating on its hinges.

Suddenly the neigh of a horse, from beyond the wall, rang out.

The two men started and trembled.

"It is nothing, only the horses; quick, help me to carry him in!" came in a guttural whisper from the lips of Sir Murdaugh Westbrooke.

Wilde, panting and shaking in all his limbs, obeyed. The body of Earle was lifted and borne down the few steps into the vault.

"He will not live here ten minutes," muttered Wilde, staggering back. "The air is death to breathe."

"So much the better — come!"

And leaping out of the vault, the baronet gained the open air. Wilde hastily followed him, and, at a sign from his master, closed the huge door. It went to with a dull clash. The Hercules shuddered.

"Fasten the iron."

With a trembling hand, Wilde obeyed; and in a few moments the vault was heavily secured. The baronet looked on with the expression of a fiend, during the work.

"And now, come," he said; "but what is that?"

And he pointed to a shadow, passing rapidly beneath the evergreens. As he uttered the words, the shadow darted toward the wall near the horses.

"A man!—some one has seen us."

The words escaped the baronet in a horrified cry. He shuddered, and exclaïmed.

"Pursue him!—he must die, or we are lost."

Wilde had not waited for the order. With one bound he reached the wall; as he cleared it, a dark figure crossed the expanse without at a run. Wilde followed; the figure stumbled; a moment afterwards, they had clutched.

"You!" cried Wilde, recognizing the gypsy.

The vagabond made no reply.

"You saw, then?" gasped Wilde.

The words were followed by a cry from the Hercules. The gypsy had drawn his knife, and plunged it into the gamekeeper's heart

"Ah!" groaned Wilde staggering back, "I am dead! but—"

And suddenly wrenching the knife from the gypsy, he drove it into his breast.

The weapon disappeared to the hilt, which struck heavily against the gypsy's breast-bone.

"We die together at least," gasped Wilde, in a broken voice.

And he fell, dragging the gypsy.

A moment afterwards, as the baronet hastened to the spot, he half rose.

"I die," muttered Wilde — "but he too —!"

He pointed to the body of the gypsy, lying on its back with the knife buried in the breast.

As Wilde spoke, his head drooped, the death-rattle issued from his throat, and falling back, he uttered a last groan and expired.

21

CHAPTER XXIV.

THE MAN FROM WENTWORTH CASTLE.

IT was nearly midnight.

Sir Murdaugh Westbrooke was sitting in his library at Westbrooke Hall.

He seemed to have grown ten years older since the morning, and was livid.

At every instant he looked over his shoulder, and listened.

"Folly!" he suddenly exclaimed, rising and uttering a short, harsh laugh; "am I a baby to start at shadows! All is safe now! discovery is impossible. My plans succeed — nothing fails! That woman is safe on board the *Fly-by Night* now, and the marriage record is burned! That man is — "

He stopped. In spite of himself a tremor agitated him.

"He too has disappeared! Thus nothing prevents my marrying Ellinor Maverick on the day after to-morrow; and *he* will not be present any more than that woman to convict me! Yes—all is safe. I marry and I inherit the Wentworth property. The obstacles have disappeared—even Gubbs and Wilde, my tools. Gubbs will go to St. Domingo, and never more be heard of; Wilde is yonder in the wood where I dragged him and the dead gypsy. When they are found, there will be no questions. My gamekeeper has fought with a poacher, and in the affray they have both been killed!"

He sat down, pale and breathing heavily, despite his reassuring reflections.

"And yet I tremble!" he muttered; "I start at every sound!"

The hoofs of a horse were heard without. A mounted man was evidently approaching rapidly.

The baronet started up.

"Who can that be!"

As he spoke, a knock was heard at the front door, and then silence followed.

The baronet seemed paralyzed. What to do? Should he secrete himself? Who was this midnight visitor?

"I am a coward!—shadows fright me! I will face all!"

And he went and opened the front door of the house. It was necessary that he should do so. Beside Wilde there had been for weeks only an old deaf crone of a servant at the hall.

A serving man was seen at the door.

"Well?" said the baronet in a low tone.

The man's hand went to his hat.

"Has Captain Earle been here, your honor? I was sent by his lordship to ask, and say that Captain Earle, who is staying at the castle, went out for a short ride this evening, and an hour or two afterwards his horse came back without any rider. His lordship thought he might have had an accident, and something might be known of him here."

The baronet responded in a low tone.

"Why here?"

"His lordship did not say, your honor."

"Say to his lordship that I have seen nothing of Captain Earle."

The servant touched his hat and retired.

The baronet closed the door, and staggered rather than walked back to the library.

"Peril surrounds me on every side! The

ghost of that boy rises to point to the spot where he is entombed alive! Was I mad to do that? Am I then the monster of monsters?"

He fell into a seat.

"Doubtless, since I do this monstrous thing! Well, let me act out my character! I will go through now to the end! Once married, I will go abroad and only return when the viscount is dead! Dead? If he were only dead now, all were well!"

A cry of pain followed the words.

He had violently clenched his hands. The movement of that upon which the dissecting knife had inflicted the wound, caused him acute agony.

"I had forgotten that!" he muttered, gazing at the slight puncture, from which he had long removed the bandage; "who would have believed that a scratch would cause so much pain?"

He pondered for more than an hour. Then he suddenly rose.

"The die is cast! Why draw back now!" he muttered. "All is decided. In two days I shall be married and on my way to France!"

A smile of ghastly triumph distorted his lips as he spoke, and, taking a light from the table, he went to his chamber.

CHAPTER XXV.

THE WEDDING AT LLANGOLLEN.

IT was two days after these scenes.

The coast of Pembrokeshire was bathed in a flood of brilliant sunshine. The great headland above Oldport rose like a giant in the fresh light. The foam danced and sparkled; and even the sombre firs of the hills seemed more cheerful for this illumination, driving away the mists of autumn.

At Llangollen church in the hills, a large crowd had assembled. It was the day of Sir Murdaugh Westbrooke's marriage to Miss Ellinor Maverick.

The selection of Llangollen church as the scene of the marriage ceremony had been made at the last moment, and in spite of the baronet's persistent objections. The fair Ellinor, however, had not been his opponent in the discussion. The old dowager, Lady Worsham, at whose house the young lady had "taken refuge," as she said, had been seized with a fit of piety or religious etiquette, it seemed; and under the influence of this sentiment she had obstinately announced that the wedding feast might be at her house, but the ceremony must be at Llangollen church.

The old dowager had triumphed. The baronet found her immovable, and with fear and trembling yielded.

"After all," he said to himself, "what have I to fear? A ghost? — men do not live two days in —"

The words died away in his throat.

"So be it, madam," he said.

And bowing sullenly, he went to make his preparations.

The morning came, and the announcement of the intended ceremony had drawn a great crowd, both of the gentry and the plainer people. Chariots stopped at the gate, and discharged their burdens of lord and lady. A crowd watched there, moving unquietly to and fro in front of the gateway. Among the crowd were seen many of the fraternity of the wolves, — rough figures, brought thither by some stronger sentiment, it seemed, than curiosity, and whose eyes were fixed on the pageant with ill-concealed hostility.

At last the chariot of Lady Worsham, containing the dowager, Sir Murdaugh Westbrooke, and Miss Ellinor Maverick drove up to the gateway.

From it issued, first, the baronet, clad with unusual splendor, but as pale as death. Then came the ladies: they entered the church, and a great crowd surged in after them.

In front of the altar stood the priest in his black canonicals. The bridal party — if that could be called a party consisting of but two or three persons — ascended the aisle, took their positions before the priest, and the ceremony was about to begin.

From the body of the church, gloomy, in spite of the sunshine, a great crowd followed the details of the scene, with varied emotions.

Many were there from simple curiosity. Others came from want of means to otherwise kill the time. Others, — and they were numerous — gazed with ill-concealed hostility on the pale bridegroom. Never popular, or personally attractive, the baronet had now few well-wishers, and was so livid as to appear hideous.

One thing about him everybody observed—his head hung down, and moved from side to side. As it thus moved, wary and fearful glances shot from beneath his gray eyebrows; more than once he looked furtively over his shoulder as though fearful of something. As he took his place beside the beautiful Ellinor, he was observed to shudder.

She was radiant, and her splendid costume set off her dazzling and magnetic beauty. It was plain that no doubts or misgivings affected *her.* She was about to become the wife of a man of great wealth and high rank — her worldly ambition was soon to be fully gratified; and in the dark eyes of the fair Ellinor, as she rustled up to the chancel, in her grand white satin, could be read haughty triumph, and the fruition of all her hopes.

The ceremony began. As it did so, a murmur issued from the crowd. They were saying to each other, " How beautiful ! " and " How hideous ! "

But Sir Murdaugh Westbrooke did not hear them. All his powers seemed to be concentrated into the one faculty of listening. His face resembled the drawn and parchment-like outlines of a corpse. He plainly feared something — some miracle, it might be — the invisible fate seemed approaching.

It came.

The priest proceeded with the ceremony, and reached the passage.

"Into this holy estate these two persons present come now to be joined."

He looked up from the book.

"If any man can show just cause why they may not lawfully be joined together, let him now speak, or hereafter forever hold his peace."

As the words issued from the priest's lips, a woman in a black dress advanced slowly up the aisle. All saw her coming, and a hundred eyes were directed toward her.

The priest gazed at her in utter astonishment. The hand containing the prayer-book sunk to his side.

The woman came on, slow, silent, with the noiseless tread of a ghost.

Suddenly the baronet raised his head. His startled eyes roamed from side to side. He glanced over his shoulder. As he did so, he uttered a low cry.

"There is just cause," said the recluse, in a low, clear voice, "why Sir Murdaugh West-brooke should not marry. I am Lady West-brooke. Here is the record of my marriage."

And she extended toward the priest the fragments of the leaf of the marriage register stolen from Martigny.

CHAPTER XXVI.

THE VENGEANCE OF A BLOOD-HOUND.

SIR MURDAUGH WESTBROOKE tottered, and leaned on the chancel railing.

Ellinor Maverick uttered a low scream, and fell back fainting in the arms of Lady Worsham.

The crowd in the body of the church rose, and towering above them could be seen the commanding figure of the Viscount Cecil, who made a gesture to some one and said coldly, —

"The moment has come!"

Then a shudder ran through the assembly. It opened right and left, and through the space thus made advanced a procession of the wolves, bearing on their shoulders —

EARLE!

The young man was wasted to a shadow. His face was paler than ashes. His eyes were sunken and bloodshot. He lay on the brawny shoulders of his brother wolves, as weak as a sick child, and as he was borne up the aisle fixed his eyes on the baronet, and whispered rather than said, —

" That is he."

The priest advanced hurriedly.

" What means this scene ? Who is this sick man ? "

" Ask the witness I have brought here." said the viscount.

And he pointed to the rear of the strange procession.

Supported between two of the wolves, was seen the gypsy, as pale and wasted as Earle. His eyes alone seemed alive as he staggered on between his two supporters, and those eyes, dark and fiery, were fixed upon the countenance of the baronet.

The priest uttered an exclamation.

" My lord ! the meaning of all this ! " he faltered.

" It means that the person whom you see there, has attempted both bigamy and murder," said the viscount.

And with his arm extended at full length, he pointed straight toward Sir Murdaugh Westbrooke.

" Do you doubt ? look at him ! "

And his extended arm remained motionless.

" Did I need the testsmony of his face, that would convict him ! " said the viscount slowly and solemnly. " But that is not needed. There are witnesses, Listen ! people of Pembrokeshire ! "

And turning to the crowd, —

" Sir Murdaugh Westbrooke married . in France — and there is his wife. He attempts to marry again, and has stolen the record — there it is. He stole my child — the only child of my poor wife who died twenty years since — to inherit from me, and buried that child alive — there he is ! But two days since all this was arranged, as he supposed, securely. The first wife was sent toward the coast to be carried abroad, and I met and was appealed to by her. The child — my child — was knocked down and dragged to this very spot, and buried alive in the Maverick vaults, by the murderer of Giles Maverick ; and a poor gypsy who saw the infamy, and was left as they thought dead, dragged his bleeding body to Oldport,

where he gave the alarm to the brave chief of
the wolves there. They came and rescued him,
almost dying ! There he is !"

He pointed to Earle.

An immense shout rose from the assembly.

"Death ! death to him !" cried the wolves ;
"he tried to murder a wolf ! Death to the
murderer !"

As they spoke, they rushed straight on the
baronet, Goliath at their head.

"Death ! death !" rose in hoarse thunder
from the ferocious crowd.

And they were about to tear the baronet to
pieces.

Suddenly Goliath recoiled, and the crowd
behind him, felt the pressure of his huge bulk.

"Look at him ! look at the murderer !" he
growled in terrified tones, pointing to the baronet.

The sight was terrible indeed.

Sir Murdaugh Westbrooke foamed at the
mouth, and his huge red tongue was hanging
out. His eyes glared around him with a vacant
and animal expression. All at once he began
to pant quickly, as a dog does when he is heated,
then he snapped, uttered a growl, which ended
in a sound like a bark, and rushed straight upon

the crowd, who gave way with terror, as he came.

"The mad dog! He was bitten!—his bite is deadly!"

Some one uttered those words.

Their effect was instant.

The crowd recoiled, and leaped over the backs of the seats, to avoid him.

He did not attempt to follow them. They seemed to have disappeared from his view. The wretched man, who had inoculated his blood with the mad dog's virus, when he punctured his hand, in dissecting the corpse, bitten by the animal, was now fully mastered by the poison, and turned into a beast. Hydrophobia — that most awful of human scourges — had clutched him. He saw nothing, heard nothing, rushed on, he knew not whither, snaping, and uttering hoarse cries. When he was followed into the churchyard, it was seen that he made for the Maverick vault.

"There are two men murdered here! One is alive!" he growled, tearing at the huge stone.

Four men threw themselves upon him, and seized him. They were scarce able to hold him. Tetanus had set in with mortal violence;

and he was borne foaming, raving, and struggling to Westbrooke hall.

Three more paroxysms assailed the miserable
man before midnight.

As the last died away, he fell back a corpse
in the arms of his attendants.

The dog of the murdered man, Giles Maverick, had avenged his master. He had bitten
and poisoned the wolf; and the dead wolf had
poisoned the murderer.

The gallows was spared the trouble. Hydrophobia ended all.

22

CHAPTER XXVII.

THE WOLVES CELEBRATE THE MARRIAGE OF THEIR CHIEF.

OUR narrative might here appropriately end, but a few words more may interest the reader.

As the baronet rushed from Llangollen Church, Ellinor Maverick was borne out fainting, by Lady Worsham; and a month afterwards they went abroad, returning only some years afterwards to Pembrokeshire.

Earle, his mother, and the gypsy were led forth in triumph by the wolves — and as the young man raised his head in the fresh sunshine, he felt his father's arms around him.

Thereat the wolves uttered a shout.

"It be his son! the son of the good viscount! he be the chief of the wolves!" shouted Goliath.

And again they caught up Earle and bore him to the viscount's coach, on their shoulders, in triumph.

"You be the chief, master, remember!" repeated Goliath.

And he uttered a second shout. The wolves howled in response, and the sound rang through the hills like thunder.

It was still reverberating in the fir-clad gorges, when the chariot with Earle, his mother, the gypsy, and the viscount, disappeared.

In an hour they were at Wentworth Castle.

. . . .

A year after these events, Edmond, son of the Viscount Cecil, was married to Rose Maverick, at Maverick House.

Lady Westbrooke remained at Wentworth Castle. Nothing could induce her to inhabit her dower estate of Westbrooke Hall.

Arthur Maverick remained unmarried. Ellinor returned only some years afterwards, and never appeared in society; dedicating her time to Lady Worsham, from whom she expected to inherit an estate.

The gypsy, promoted to the post of head

gamekeeper at Wentworth Castle, lived and died, loved and trusted by Earle.

So terminated the drama — such were the fates of the personages.

The Viscount Cecil seemed, more than all others, content with the denouement. He had regained his son, and that son was married to his favorite Rose.

The wedding was a grand one. No less a person than Lieutenant Dargonne made his appearance, and laughed and drank his old captain's health. Then the cortège set out from Maverick House for Wentworth Castle. As it approached Oldport, an ovation awaited it. The wolves attacked it all at once, with loud cries.

The horses were taken from the chariot containing Earle and his blushing bride; brawny hands seized the vehicle and drew it on amid cries of rejoicing. And above the ferocious crowd, with bearded faces and brandished arms, rose the shout of Goliath, —

"He be the chief of the wolves!"

THE END.

A Catalogue of
BOOKS
ISSUED BY
CARLETON,
NEW YORK.
Madison Square,
corner of
5th Avenue and Broadway.
1871.

" *There is a kind of physiognomy in the titles of books no less than in the faces of men, by which a skilful observer will know as well what to expect from the one as the other.*"—BUTLER.

NEW BOOKS

And New Editions Recently Issued by
CARLETON, Publisher, New York,

Madison Square, corner Fifth Av. and Broadway.]

N. B.—THE PUBLISHERS, upon receipt of the price in advance, will send any of the following Books by mail, POSTAGE FREE, to any part of the United States. This convenient and very safe mode may be adopted when the neighboring Booksellers are not supplied with the desired work.   State name and address in full.

Marion Harland's Works.

ALONE.—	A novel.	12mo. cloth,	$1.50
HIDDEN PATH.—	do.	do.	$1.50
MOSS SIDE.—	do.	do.	$1.50
NEMESIS.—	do.	do.	$1.50
MIRIAM.—	do.	do.	$1.50
AT LAST.—	do. *Just Published.*		$1.50
HELEN GARDNER'S WEDDING-DAY.—		do.	$1.50
SUNNYBANK.—	do.	do.	$1.50
HUSBANDS AND HOMES.—	do.	do.	$1.50
RUBY'S HUSBAND.—	do.	do.	$1.50
PHEMIE'S TEMPTATION.—		do.	$1.50

Miss Muloch.

JOHN HALIFAX.—A novel. With illustration.	12mo. cloth,	$1.75
A LIFE FOR A LIFE.—	do.	do.	$1.75

Charlotte Bronte (Currer Bell).

JANE EYRE.—A novel. With illustration.	12mo. cloth,	$1.75
THE PROFESSOR.— do.	do.	do.	$1.75
SHIRLEY.— do.	do.	do.	$1.75
VILLETTE.— do.	do.	do.	$1.75

Hand-Books of Society.

THE HABITS OF GOOD SOCIETY ; thoughts, hints, and anecdotes, concerning nice points of taste, good manners, and the art of making oneself agreeable.   .   . 12mo. cloth, $1.75

THE ART OF CONVERSATION.—A sensible and instructive work, that ought to be in the hands of every one who wishes to be either an agreeable talker or listener. 12mo. cloth, $1.50

ARTS OF WRITING, READING, AND SPEAKING.—An excellent book for self-instruction and improvement. 12mo. cloth, $1.50

HAND-BOOKS OF SOCIETY.—The above three choice volumes bound in extra style, full gilt ornamental back, uniform in appearance, and in a handsome box.   .   .   . $5.00

Mrs. Mary J. Holmes' Works.

'LENA RIVERS.—	A novel.	12mo. cloth,	$1.50
DARKNESS AND DAYLIGHT.—	do.	do.	$1.50
TEMPEST AND SUNSHINE.—	do.	do.	$1.50
MARIAN GREY.—	do.	do.	$1.50
MEADOW BROOK.—	do.	do.	$1 50
ENGLISH ORPHANS.—	do.	do.	$1.53
DORA DEANE.—	do.	do.	$1.53
COUSIN MAUDE.—	do.	do.	$1.50
HOMESTEAD ON THE HILLSIDE.—	do.	do.	$1.50
HUGH WORTHINGTON.—	do.	do.	$1.50
THE CAMERON PRIDE.—	do.	do.	$1.50
ROSE MATHER.—	do.	do.	$1.50
ETHELYN'S MISTAKE.—*Just Published.* do.	do.		$1.50

Miss Augusta J. Evans.

BEULAH.—A novel of great power.		12mo. cloth,	$1.75
MACARIA.— do. do.		do.	$1.75
ST. ELMO.— do. do.		do.	$2.00
VASHTI.— do. do. *Just Published.*	do		$2.00

Victor Hugo.

LES MISÉRABLES.—The celebrated novel.   One large 8vo volume, paper covers, $2.00 ;   .   .   .   cloth bound, $2.50
LES MISÉRABLES.—Spanish. Two vols., paper, $4.00 ; cl., $5.00

Mrs. A. P. Hill.

MRS. HILL'S NEW COOKERY BOOK, and receipts.   .   .$2.00

Algernon Charles Swinburne.

LAUS VENERIS, AND OTHER POEMS.—   .   12mo. cloth, $1.75

Captain Mayne Reid's Works—Illustrated.

THE SCALP HUNTERS.—	A romance.	12mo. cloth,	$1.50
THE RIFLE RANGERS.—	do.	do.	$1.50
THE TIGER HUNTER.—	do.	do.	$1.50
OSCEOLA, THE SEMINOLE.—	do.	do.	$1.50
THE WAR TRAIL.—	do.	do	$1.50
THE HUNTER'S FEAST.—	do.	do.	$1.50
RANGERS AND REGULATORS.—	do.	do.	$1.50
THE WHITE CHIEF.—	do.	do.	$1.50
THE QUADROON.—	do.	do.	$1.50
THE WILD HUNTRESS.—	do	do.	$1.50
THE WOOD RANGERS.—	do.	do.	$1.50
WILD LIFE.—	do.	do.	$1 50
THE MAROON.—	do.	do.	$1.50
LOST LEONORE.—	do.	do.	$1.50
THE HEADLESS HORSEMAN.— do.		do.	$1.50
THE WHITE GAUNTLET.— *Just Published.*		do.	$1.50

A. S. Roe's Works.

A LONG LOOK AHEAD.— A novel.	.	12mo. cloth, $1.50
TO LOVE AND TO BE LOVED.— do.	. .	do. $1.50
TIME AND TIDE.— do.	. .	do. $1.50
I'VE BEEN THINKING.— do.	. .	do. $1.50
THE STAR AND THE CLOUD.— do.	. .	do. $1.50
TRUE TO THE LAST.— do.	. .	do. $1.50
HOW COULD HE HELP IT?— do.	. .	do. $1.50
LIKE AND UNLIKE.— do.	. .	do. $1.50
LOOKING AROUND.— do.	. .	do. $1.50
WOMAN OUR ANGEL.— do.	. .	do. $1.50
THE CLOUD ON THE HEART.—*Just published.*		do. $1.50

Richard B. Kimball.

WAS HE SUCCESSFUL?— A novel.	. .	12mo. cloth, $1.75
UNDERCURRENTS.— do.	. .	do. $1.75
SAINT LEGER.— do.	. .	do. $1.75
ROMANCE OF STUDENT LIFE.—do.	. .	do. $1.75
IN THE TROPICS.— do.	. .	do. $1.75
HENRY POWERS, Banker. do.	. .	do. $1.75
TO-DAY.—A novel. *Just published.*	.	do. $1.75

Joseph Rodman Drake.

THE CULPRIT FAY.—A faery poem, with 100 illustrations.	$2.00
DO. Superbly bound in turkey morocco.	$5.00

"Brick" Pomeroy.

SENSE.—An illustrated vol. of fireside musings.	12mo. cl., $1.50
NONSENSE.— do. do. comic sketches.	do. $1.50
OUR SATURDAY NIGHTS. do. . pathos and sentiment.	$1.50

Comic Books—Illustrated.

ARTEMUS WARD, His Book.—Letters, etc.	12mo. cl.,	$1.50
DO. His Travels—Mormons, etc.	do.	$1.50
DO. In London.—Punch Letters.	do.	$1.50
DO. His Panorama and Lecture.	do.	$1.50
DO. Sandwiches for Railroad.	. . .	25
JOSH BILLINGS ON ICE, and other things.—	12mo. cl.,	$1.50
DO. His Book of Proverbs, etc.	do.	$1.50
DO. Farmer's Allmanax. *Just published.*		.25
FANNY FERN.—Folly as it Flies.	. . . .	$1.50
DO. Gingersnaps	. . . . .	$1.50
VERDANT GREEN.—A racy English college story.	12mo. cl.,	$1.50
CONDENSED NOVELS, ETC.—By F. Bret Harte.	do.	$1.50
MILES O'REILLY.—His Book of Adventures.	do.	$1.50
ORPHEUS C. KERR.—Kerr Papers, 3 vols.	do.	$1.50
DO. Avery Glibun. A novel.	. .	$2.00
DO. Smoked Glass.	. 12mo. cl.,	$1.50

Children's Books—Illustrated.

THE ART OF AMUSING.—With 150 illustrations. 12mo. cl., $1.50
FRIENDLY COUNSEL FOR GIRLS.—A charming book. do. $1.50
THE CHRISTMAS FONT.—By Mary J. Holmes.   do. $1.00
ROBINSON CRUSOE.—A Complete edition.   .   do. $1.50
LOUIE'S LAST TERM.—By author "Rutledge."   do. $1.75
ROUNDHEARTS, and other stories.—   do.   .   do. $1.75
PASTIMES WITH MY LITTLE FRIENDS.—   .   .   do. $1.50
WILL-O'-THE-WISP.—From the German.   .   do. $1.53

M. Michelet's Remarkable Works.

LOVE (L'AMOUR).—Translated from the French. 12mo. cl., $1.50
WOMAN (LA FEMME).—   .   do.   .   .   do. $1.50

Ernest Renan.

THE LIFE OF JESUS.—Translated from the French. 12mo.cl., $1.75
THE APOSTLES.—   .   .   do.   .   .   do. $1.75
SAINT PAUL.—   .   .   do.   .   .   do. $1.75

Popular Italian Novels.

DOCTOR ANTONIO.—A love story.   By Ruffini.   12mo. cl., $1.75
BEATRICE CENCI.—By Guerrazzi, with portrait.   do. $1.75

Rev. John Cumming, D.D., of London.

THE GREAT TRIBULATION.—Two series.   12mo. cloth, $1.50
THE GREAT PREPARATION.—   do.   .   do. $1.50
THE GREAT CONSUMMATION.   do.   .   do. $1.50
THE LAST WARNING CRY.—   .   .   do. $1.50

Mrs. Ritchie (Anna Cora Mowatt).

FAIRY FINGERS.—A capital new novel.   .   12mo. cloth, $1.75
THE MUTE SINGER.—   do.   .   do. $1.75
THE CLERGYMAN'S WIFE—and other stories.   do. $1.75

T. S. Arthur's New Works.

LIGHT ON SHADOWED PATHS.—A novel.   12mo. cloth, $1.50
OUT IN THE WORLD.—   .   do.   .   .   do. $1.50

WHAT CAME AFTERWARDS.—   do.   .   .   do. $1.50
OUR NEIGHBORS.—   .   do.   .   .   do. $1.50

Geo. W. Carleton.

OUR ARTIST IN CUBA.—With 50 comic illustrations.   . $1.50
OUR ARTIST IN PERU.—   do.   do.   .   . $1.50
OUR ARTIST IN AFRICA.—(*In press*)   do.   . $1.50

John Esten Cooke.

FAIRFAX.—   A brilliant new novel.   .   12mo. cloth, $1.50
HILT TO HILT.—   do.   .   .   .   do. $1.50
HAMMER AND RAPIER.—   do.   .   .   .   do. $1.50
OUT OF THE FOAM.—   do.   *In press.*   do. $1.50

How to Make Money

AND HOW TO KEEP IT.—A practical, readable book, that ought to be in the hands of every person who wishes to earn money or to keep what he has. One of the best books ever published. By Thomas A. Davies.   12mo. cloth, $1.50

J. Cordy Jeaffreson.

A BOOK ABOUT LAWYERS.—A collection of interesting anec-dotes and incidents connected with the most distinguished members of the Legal Profession. . 12mo. cloth, $2.00

Fred. Saunders.

WOMAN, LOVE, AND MARRIAGE.—A charming volume about three most fascinating topics. . . 12mo. cloth, $1.50

Edmund Kirke.

AMONG THE PINES.—Or Life in the South. 12mo. cloth, $1.50
MY SOUTHERN FRIENDS.—   do. . . do. $1.50
DOWN IN TENNESSEE.—   do. . . do. $1.50
ADRIFT IN DIXIE.—   do. . . do. $1.50
AMONG THE GUERILLAS.—   do. . . do. $1.50

Charles Reade.

THE CLOISTER AND THE HEARTH.—A magnificent new novel—the best this author ever wrote. . 8vo. cloth, $2.00

The Opera.

TALES FROM THE OPERAS.—A collection of clever stories, based upon the plots of all the famous operas. 12mo. cloth, $1.50

Robert B. Roosevelt.

THE GAME-FISH OF THE NORTH.—Illustrated. 12mo. cloth, $2.00
SUPERIOR FISHING.—   do.   do. $2.00
THE GAME-BIRDS OF THE NORTH.— . . do. $2.00

By the Author of "Rutledge."

RUTLEDGE.—A deeply interesting novel. 12mo. cloth, $1.75
THE SUTHERLANDS.—   do. . . do. . $1.75
FRANK WARRINGTON.—   do. . . do. . $1.75
ST. PHILIP'S.—   do. . . do. . $1.75
LOUIE'S LAST TERM AT ST. MARY'S.— . do. . $1.75
ROUNDHEARTS AND OTHER STORIES.—For children. do. . $1.75
A ROSARY FOR LENT.—Devotional Readings.   do. . $1.75

Love in Letters.

A collection of piquant love-letters. . 12mo. cloth, $2.00

Dr. J. J. Craven.

THE PRISON-LIFE OF JEFFERSON DAVIS.— . 12mo. cloth, $2.00

Walter Barrett, Clerk.

THE OLD MERCHANTS OF NEW YORK.—   Five vols. cloth, $10.

H. T. Sperry.

COUNTRY LOVE *vs.* CITY FLIRTATION.— . 12mo. cloth, $2.00

Miscellaneous Works.

CHRIS AND OTHO.—A novel by Mrs. Julie P. Smith. .	$1 75
CROWN JEWELS.— do. Mrs. Emma L. Moffett.	$1 75
ADRIFT WITH A VENGEANCE.— Kinahan Cornwallis. .	$1.50
THE FRANCO-PRUSSIAN WAR IN 1870.—By W. D. Landon.	
DREAM MUSIC.—Poems by Frederic Rowland Marvin. .	$1.50
RAMBLES IN CUBA.—By an American Lady. . .	$1.50
BEHIND THE SCENES, in the White House.—Keckley. .	$2.00
YACHTMAN'S PRIMER.—For Amateur Sailors.—Warren.	50
RURAL ARCHITECTURE.—By M. Field. With illustrations.	$2.00
TREATISE ON DEAFNESS.—By Dr. E. B. Lighthill. . .	$1.50
WOMEN AND THEATRES.—A new book, by Olive Logan.	$1.50
WARWICK.—A new novel by Mansfield Tracy Walworth.	$1.75
SIBYL HUNTINGTON.—A novel by Mrs. J. C. R. Dorr. .	$1.75
LIVING WRITERS OF THE SOUTH.—By Prof. Davidson. .	$2.00
STRANGE VISITORS.—A book from the Spirit World. .	$1.50
UP BROADWAY, and its Sequel.—A story by Eleanor Kirk.	$1.50
MILITARY RECORD, of Appointments in the U.S. Army.	$5.00
HONOR BRIGHT.—A new American novel. . . .	$1.50
MALBROOK.— do. do. do. . . .	$1.50
GUILTY OR NOT GUILTY.— do. do. . . .	$1.75
ROBERT GREATHOUSE.—A new novel by John F. Swift .	$2.00
THE GOLDEN CROSS, and poems by Irving Van Wart, jr.	$1.50
ATHALIAH.—A new novel by Joseph H. Greene, jr. .	$1.75
REGINA, and other poems.—By Eliza Cruger. . .	$1.50
THE WICKEDEST WOMAN IN NEW YORK.—By C. H. Webb.	50
MONTALBAN.—A new American novel. . . .	$1.75
MADEMOISELLE MERQUEM.—A novel by George Sand. .	$1.75
THE IMPENDING CRISIS OF THE SOUTH.—By H. R. Helper.	$2.00
NOJOQUE—A Question for a Continent.— do. .	$2.00
PARIS IN 1867.—By Henry Morford.	$1.75
THE BISHOP'S SON.—A novel by Alice Cary. . .	$1.75
CRUISE OF THE ALABAMA AND SUMTER.—By Capt. Semmes.	$1.50
HELEN COURTENAY.—A novel, author " Vernon Grove."	$1.75
SOUVENIRS OF TRAVEL.—By Madame Octavia W. LeVert.	$2.00
VANQUISHED.—A novel by Agnes Leonard. . .	$1.75
WILL-O'-THE-WISP.—A child's book, from the German .	$1.50
FOUR OAKS.—A novel by Kamba Thorpe. . . .	$1.75
THE CHRISTMAS FONT.—A child's book, by M. J. Holmes.	$1.00
POEMS, BY SARAH T. BOLTON.	$1.50
MARY BRANDEGEE—A novel by Cuyler Pine. . .	$1.75
RENSHAWE.— do. do. . . .	$1.75
MOUNT CALVARY.—By Matthew Hale Smith. . .	$2.00
PROMETHEUS IN ATLANTIS.—A prophecy. . . .	$2.00
TITAN AGONISTES.—An American novel. . . .	$2.00

www.ingramcontent.com/pod-product-compliance
Lightning Source LLC
Chambersburg PA
CBHW021800110726
47902CB00006B/1594